Claymore the stairwell

But Bolan was prepared for them. He skirted the stairs until the banister was at chest height, then hopped over the railing, well out of the effective kill zone of the explosives. The balcony was clear. A set of double doors took him to an anteroom.

The sentry stationed there was pressed against the wall, opposite the door. As the terrorist leveled his shotgun, Bolan swiveled, bringing up the M4.

The shotgun roared, the impact slamming into Bolan's gut like a hammer blow. Air rushed from his lungs and he went down, landing on his back, hard.

Then all he could see was the barrel of the shotgun. The neo-Nazi racked the pump action. "Bye-bye, asshole."

MACK BOLAN ®
The Executioner

The Executioner®
Don Pendleton's
FINAL JUDGMENT

A GOLD EAGLE BOOK FROM
WORLDWIDE®

TORONTO • NEW YORK • LONDON
AMSTERDAM • PARIS • SYDNEY • HAMBURG
STOCKHOLM • ATHENS • TOKYO • MILAN
MADRID • WARSAW • BUDAPEST • AUCKLAND

Recycling programs
for this product may
not exist in your area.

First edition July 2012

ISBN-13: 978-0-373-64404-9

Special thanks and acknowledgment to
Phil Elmore for his contribution to this work.

FINAL JUDGMENT

Printed in U.S.A.

The rifle…has no moral stature. Naturally, it may be used by evil men for evil purposes, but there are more good men than evil, and while the latter cannot be persuaded to the path of righteousness by propaganda, they can certainly be corrected by good men with rifles.

—John Dean "Jeff" Cooper
1920–2006

Every man confronted with the need to correct a terrible wrong—to strike back at those who've taken his blood, destroyed his life—must choose. He can choose the path of revenge or he can choose the path of justice.

—Mack Bolan

THE
MACK BOLAN
LEGEND

Nothing less than a war could have fashioned the destiny of the man called Mack Bolan. Bolan earned the Executioner title in the jungle hell of Vietnam.

But this soldier also wore another name—Sergeant Mercy. He was so tagged because of the compassion he showed to wounded comrades-in-arms and Vietnamese civilians.

Mack Bolan's second tour of duty ended prematurely when he was given emergency leave to return home and bury his family, victims of the Mob. Then he declared a one-man war against the Mafia.

He confronted the Families head-on from coast to coast, and soon a hope of victory began to appear. But Bolan had broken society's every rule. That same society started gunning for this elusive warrior—to no avail.

So Bolan was offered amnesty to work within the system against terrorism. This time, as an employee of Uncle Sam, Bolan became Colonel John Phoenix. With a command center at Stony Man Farm in Virginia, he and his new allies—Able Team and Phoenix Force—waged relentless war on a new adversary: the KGB.

But when his one true love, April Rose, died at the hands of the Soviet terror machine, Bolan severed all ties with Establishment authority.

Now, after a lengthy lone-wolf struggle and much soul-searching, the Executioner has agreed to enter an "arm's-length" alliance with his government once more, reserving the right to pursue personal missions in his Everlasting War.

1

Mack Bolan chopped the sentry in the throat with the edge of his hand. The neo-Nazi, clad in camouflage fatigues, made choking, gurgling noises as he collapsed to his knees, his eyes wide. The plea on his face was obvious.

Bolan smashed his elbow in and down. The sentry collapsed in a tortured heap on the floor of the stairwell. The man still known to a select few as the Executioner deftly plucked a Kalashnikov rifle from the neo-Nazi's grip, popped the cover and removed the bolt. He tossed the latter down the steps and left the disabled weapon with the unconscious man—but not before zip-tying the sentry's hands and feet and running two layers of black gaffer tape across the man's mouth.

Then Bolan waited.

Few men could be truly still when they needed to be. Mack Bolan was a master, and now he waited to see if the noise of his covert insertion had alerted anyone else. The access door he had used to gain entry to the District of Columbia courthouse had been guarded from without as well as by the sentry he had just removed, but the terrorists were expecting a SWAT incursion or some other force to attack en masse. They weren't prepared for a single man, because in their minds one armed man wasn't a threat.

They were wrong.

Bolan carried his standard complement of weaponry over his combat blacksuit and attached to his web gear. His suppressed and custom-tuned Beretta 93-R machine pistol rode in the shoulder holster under his left arm; his .44 Magnum Desert Eagle pistol rode in his waistband behind his right hip, snug in a Kydex friction-fit scabbard. On his web gear, inverted for a fast draw, was a combat dagger with a tapered, rubber-coated handle and an upswept, razor-sharp blade. The knife was the length of Bolan's forearm.

Across his chest he wore a canvas war bag bearing more munitions and combat items, while slung on his body in a single-point harness was a heavily modified M-4 carbine. The cut-down assault rifle bore red-dot optics, and an adapted M-203 grenade launcher was slung beneath its barrel. It was also capable of full-automatic fire, not just 3-round bursts, thanks to the tender ministrations of John "Cowboy" Kissinger, the Stony Man Farm's armorer. Not for the first time it occurred to Bolan that, were he ever to cut ties with the Farm and the Sensitive Operations Group, he would genuinely miss the toys.

It was Hal Brognola, director of SOG, who had dispatched the Executioner on this mission. The call, scrambled through Bolan's secure satellite-capable smartphone, held an edge of urgency that immediately triggered the soldier's combat instincts.

"Striker," Brognola had said, using Bolan's code name, "our justice system is under attack."

This was a sensitive point for the big Fed, for Brognola operated under the auspices of the Justice Department. Bolan knew his old friend would take very seriously any threat to the system he and the counterterror operatives of Stony Man Farm worked so hard to protect.

"I'm listening, Hal," Bolan had said.

"Klaus Reinhardt Nitzche," Brognola said, practically spitting each word. "Heard of him?"

"That's the old Nazi concentration camp guard they just caught in Buenos Aires, isn't it?"

"Nitzche was more than just a guard," Brognola said. "He was the provisional camp commander of Schlechterwald, one of the more obscure but vile death camps established in the waning days of World War II. According to records recovered after the camp's liberation, Nitzche assassinated the camp's SS leader and assumed his place because Nitzche believed the SS was too soft on the prisoners. He remained in place until Hitler's suicide, disappearing sometime during the chaos surrounding the end of the war and the collapse of Nazi Germany."

"Sounds like a beautiful human being."

"He was a monster," Brognola said. "Rumor has it that he kept a very detailed diary, some pages of which he copied into the camp's logs. Those logs, recovered by American forces who assaulted the camp, detail atrocities you cannot imagine, Striker."

Bolan said nothing to that. He had seen plenty of atrocities in his endless war. He doubted there was much a human being could do to violate another that he hadn't encountered, but the Nazis had proved extremely imaginative on that score.

"Do you recall," Brognola said, "the Holocaust remembrance program broadcast nationally last fall?"

"I don't get to watch a lot of television," Bolan said.

"The program was notable," the Fed explained, "because it featured a recorded interview with Eli Berwald. Berwald was a youth when he and his parents were imprisoned and tortured in Schlechterwald."

"He'd have to be…"

"He's pushing eighty," Brognola said, "and not in the best of health. But his mind is strong, as is his passion for revenge. He said as much in the interview, which was taped only weeks before Berwald's organization, Lantern, brought the eighty-eight-year-old Nitzche kicking and screaming from Argentina."

"They extracted him?" Bolan asked.

"They kidnapped him," Brognola said. "Once they had him in the U.S., their legal team jumped through a bunch of hoops. I won't bore you with all the bureaucratic maneuvers involved. Suffice it to say they eventually had Nitzche processed through our legal system and charged with war crimes. The trial, a real televised circus, was to start today. It was going to be a message, a final blow to the last bastions of World War II. To war criminals, should any be alive and lurking out there today. Lantern has issued several press releases to that effect. Justice Has a Long Memory is their slogan."

"They have a lot of pull for lobbyists."

"Lantern is not simply a Jewish activist group," Brognola said. "It borders on a vigilante organization. They are extremely militant and completely unapologetic about their activities. Much more so in recent years than in the past, but there it is."

"Can you blame them?" Bolan asked.

"No," Brognola said. "But that doesn't change the complications this raises."

"Such as?"

"Berwald's Lantern is led primarily by his son, Eli Berwald Jr., known as Aaron to his friends and family. The elder Berwald operates in an advisory capacity, but Aaron is a firebrand. He's run afoul of weapons charges twice, although both times, strings have been pulled behind the scenes to get him off. His father has powerful friends within the government, as you might expect. Berwald Sr. is no stranger to the games we play here in Washington."

"And?" Bolan prompted.

"Lantern paid a celebrity bounty hunter some outrageous fee to go into Argentina and kidnap Nitzche," Brognola said. "You probably haven't seen the guy's reality-television program."

"I can't say I have."

"Nitzche was almost killed during the illegal extradition," Brognola said. "Several men were injured. The bounty hunter is now wanted in Argentina, which is irrelevant, but the fact that Nitzche was guarded by armed men is what makes this complicated. These men were members of a secretive neo-Nazi group called Heil Nitzche, which Klaus Nitzche has been operating under the radar since he went to ground in Buenos Aires all those years ago. I've had the team at the Farm digging through the records, now that we know what to look for. The pattern painted is alarming. Heil Nitzche has funding, they have equipment and they have balls. And as of half past eight this morning, they have an entire courthouse right here in Wonderland."

"A terrorist assault," Bolan said.

"Yes," Brognola said. "Nitzche and his HN thugs have seized the building and taken the judge, the jury and the gallery hostage. They've got automatic weapons and, we believe, explosives. They're demanding safe passage by helicopter out of D.C., and if they don't get it by their deadline this afternoon, they're going to start killing hostages. Several court security officers have already been killed."

"Which is where I come in," Bolan stated.

"Absolutely," Brognola said. "The Man asked for you specifically, and if he hadn't, I would have pushed for it. We need you to do what D.C. SWAT personnel and perhaps even Able Team wouldn't be able to do. A single man may be able to get inside that building and take them down from within. If we mount a coordinated assault, it will quickly become a massacre."

"Get me there," Bolan said. "I'll do it."

"G-Force is already on his way to your location," Brognola said, referring to the Farm's ace pilot, Jack Grimaldi, by his code name. "But this gets worse."

"Worse than a courthouse full of hostages, held by a Nazi war criminal relic backed by well-equipped enforcers?"

"Lantern is still involved," Brognola said. "Authorities manning the cordon around the courthouse have twice stopped Eli Berwald Jr. and a team of men armed only with knives. They're smart. They know that without a firearms violation there's not much we can do to hold them. The second time, the Metropolitan police took them in on tenuous trespassing charges, but that's not going to stick."

"I assume they're keen to bring Nitzche back into custody themselves?"

"Something like that." Brognola sighed. "Lord save us from zealous amateurs. They're not that far away. Lantern has a fairly impressive headquarters in Williamsburg, Virginia. While we can probably keep them from blundering past the cordon and getting themselves shot, I can't absolutely guarantee you won't trip over them at some point."

"I'll keep that in mind," Bolan said. It wouldn't do to put a bullet in a Lantern activist, after mistaking him for one of Nitzche's neo-Nazi HN goons. "Operational parameters?"

"Save the hostages," Brognola said.

"And Nitzche?"

"Your discretion. As long as he doesn't remain at large, the Man will be satisfied. And so will I."

"You got it," Bolan said.

"Striker?"

"Yeah?"

"Good hunting," the big Fed said.

"Thanks." Bolan had closed the connection, determined to get in position and get to work as soon as possible. Only moments later, he had heard the thrumming of rotor blades. That would be Jack Grimaldi and a helicopter.

The helicopter was a gunship. A care package, bearing the modified M-16 rifle and Bolan's war bag of munitions, had been aboard.

Now, only hours later, the soldier's boots were on the ground behind enemy-held territory.

He checked his smartphone's files, which Stony Man Farm's mission controller, Barbara Price, had uploaded to his phone while he was in transit to D.C. The layout of the building was simple enough. The construction was very solid— concrete, stone, marble, and reinforcements where applicable. These walls would be more resistant to gunfire than many; a pistol bullet would travel through most interior walls and even some exterior ones in a traditionally framed building. Bolan knew, too, that the sound of his steps would be amplified. He moved carefully, heel to toe, his combat boots as quiet as he could make them on the marble floors.

At the top of the stairwell he found the first claymore-style mine.

It was a few generations removed from the old Vietnam-era claymores, but the device's purpose was obvious enough. Written in German across the front of the mine were words that roughly translated to "front toward enemy." Bolan had picked up enough foreign languages through the years that he could tell that much. The mine had an amber LED that blinked once per second.

Bolan shrugged, reached down and turned it around to face the other way.

He moved to the side of the metal fire door, pressed himself against the wall and rapped quietly on the reinforced glass window. "Help!" he said quietly, hoping he was still loud enough to be heard on the other side. "I've cut myself! I think I'm bleeding out!"

The response was almost immediate. Another man in camouflage fatigues pushed the door open. His hand was still on the door lever when Bolan reached out, locking his wrist between thumb and index finger. He pulled sharply.

The surprised neo-Nazi had no time to cry out, no time to resist. He made a strange grunting cry as his brain tried to process his sudden freefall through space. Then he landed on his neck in the stairwell below. There was a sickening crunch as vertebrae snapped. The rattle of air escaping his lungs was paced by his evacuating bowels.

Bolan scanned the corpse but saw no weapon. He was holding the door open to prevent it from slamming back into place, where it would lock once more. Sticking his head through the opening, he saw another Kalashnikov leaning upright against the wall.

Amateurs, Bolan thought. He gave this weapon the same disassembly treatment he had given the previous one, separating the bolt from the assault rifle and tossing the component onto the corpse of the rifle's former owner. He left the weapon itself at the top of the stairwell, behind the door, where it couldn't be seen by casual observers from the other side.

There were two more claymore-style mines here. He picked them up, checked them, and simply flicked the switches on their electronic detonators. The amber LEDs switched off. He tucked the mines into his war bag.

Moving smoothly down the hall, checking the floor plan on his phone, Bolan caught a glimpse of movement around the corner of the corridor ahead. He ducked into an alcove that housed a trio of pay phones and a water fountain. Waiting, he heard footsteps. There were two men.

"South stairwell," one of them said. "I say again, south stairwell, this is Rover Two. Come in."

Bolan knew the stairwell where he'd made his entry faced south. No doubt these HN thugs were checking on their sentry posts—and getting no response from the pair Bolan had just sent to whatever hate-drenched Valhalla these neo-Nazis thought awaited them. When there was no response, the pair would raise an alarm. Bolan's element of surprise would evaporate.

Well, he'd known that would happen.

Quietly, the soldier popped the retaining snap on his leather shoulder holster, covering the sound with the flesh of his thumb. The Beretta 93-R machine pistol filled his hand as if custom molded to it. He flicked the selector switch to Single as the snout of the attached suppressor cleared leather. There would be a time and place for his own assault rifle, suspended from his harness on its single-point sling, but right now, he wanted quiet.

Bolan leaned out of the alcove as the pair of neo-Nazi terrorists walked past his position. They were perhaps two yards away when he extended the Beretta, lined up his sights on the head of the man with the walkie-talkie and squeezed the trigger.

The two-way radio was soaked in blood when it hit the marble floor. The corpse stood for the briefest of moments before its knees gave way and it toppled. The other sentry, whose AK was slung over his shoulder, slowly turned. The side of his face was speckled crimson.

"Call out and you're dead," Bolan warned. "Put the rifle on the floor."

"You shot him from behind," the man hissed. Shock and rage twisted his face. His eyes were wide and bloodshot.

"Does that offend your sense of honor?" Bolan asked quietly. "A terrorist holding innocent people hostage, desperate to free an old hatemonger with the torture and death of countless innocent people on his hands? *You're* upset that I didn't follow the rules?"

"Coward," the sentry said. His hand started to creep across his chest. He was going to try for the rifle. "Race traitor."

"You know what I hate most about neo-Nazis?" Bolan asked, his voice calm, just the barest hint above a whisper. "You're always convinced you're the smartest people in the room. You think you've got it all figured out, and anybody who doesn't agree with your hateful simpleton's logic must be a sellout to the bogeymen you fear."

"Zionist Jew-lover—" the neo-Nazi started to shout.

"Shut up," Bolan said, and shot him in the throat.

The sentry hit the marble. His hands went to his throat. Trying and failing to stem the flow from the wound that had choked off his words, he stared up at Bolan, then bled out.

2

Bolan made more than one circuit of the middle level of the courthouse, which opened onto a stairwell leading down to the main gallery, the doors of which were closed and chained from the outside. Four armed, camouflage-clad sentries stood with Kalashnikovs at the ready at the bottom of the semicircular stairs.

Within, Nitzche and the rest of his HN gunmen—those not detailed to secure the structure itself—would be passing the time however it suited them. Even through the thick walls of the courthouse, Bolan could hear the bullhorn-amplified shouts of hostage negotiators coming from behind the police cordon. Brognola and the Farm had provided a comprehensive report outlining what was known of the initial terrorist capture of the building. It showed an above-average level of military awareness that was reflected in the sentries' cross-patrol communication.

Bolan had no respect for neo-Nazis, but this bunch had more training than was usual, probably because Nitzche had been calling the shots while building the organization to serve him as a private army. That meant the danger they represented to Bolan, and the resistance they could offer, was correspondingly greater than other groups of white supremacists he had faced. Nitzche was, according to their files, a strong and intelligent leader. Such an individual made all the difference when rallying followers like these.

It was time to start chipping away at the opposition.

Before Bolan moved back into the corridor, he positioned his captured remote-detonation mines. Then he circled around to the access stairs that led to the rear of the court. There was a second stairway inside the court itself, accessing a balcony observation level that connected, in turn, to the roof. These were used by reporters and people who attended the proceedings, and were far more public than the stairs at the rear.

The back steps were adjacent to the judge's chambers and were, according to the plans and information sent to Bolan, used by the presiding judge if he wished to make a discreet exit to the second-floor offices.

Predictably, this access was mined, but none of the weapons bore antitamper switches, such as mercury triggers designed to detonate the device when it was disturbed. Such measures would have made short work of the counteroperation Bolan was running. His adversaries were trained, he decided, but they weren't *that* trained. He permitted himself a wry smile as he repositioned two more of the mines at the edge of the access stairs.

The neo-Nazis probably thought an assault on the building would be loud and obvious. So they'd have plenty of warning. Nitzche's people had likely planned to use the mines as a first-wave defense. They would have been effective, too, had it come to that. Brognola and the President had been correct to think one man could do what a coordinated and overwhelming use of force could not.

Such operations always entailed heavy losses. Bolan's acceptable percentage of noncombatant deaths was zero, but there were other counterterror operatives who didn't feel that way. Russian special forces had several times demonstrated that, and painfully, in one case putting down a high-profile hostage standoff using anesthetic gas. They had gassed the target building and then swept through it, checking the unconscious occupants and shooting the terrorists in the head. The tactic was brutal, efficient and very, very final.

The only problem was that the powerful gas used had caused overdose deaths in some of the civilians. Conventional force operations traditionally fared little better, even when simultaneous and coordinated guerrilla tactics were used. No, in this case, the Executioner was the hostages' best hope of walking out of court alive.

Bolan intended to see that they did, every last one of them.

He was counting on the fact that, as much as they blustered about killing their captives, the neo-Nazis needed those human shields. The hostages were the only reason the building hadn't been taken and cleared using overwhelming force. Even when the gunfire started, the terrorists would be reluctant to start shooting their only leverage. They would fear coming face-to-face with SWAT or military guns with nothing standing between them and righteous bullets.

That would be all the delay Bolan needed.

The rear door to the judge's chambers was almost hidden, flush with the wall and paneled to match it. Through the door, he could hear voices.

"—a problem," said the first man. "Several sentries aren't reporting."

"Try them again," said the second man.

"I have. No good."

Bolan placed the last of his stolen claymore-style mines in front of the concealed door. He backed away down the corridor, using the corner of the hallway to shield himself. He was exposed to either side, and was very aware that there were more neo-Nazi sentries patrolling the building. There was no helping that. When the bullets started to fly, he would rely on his training, his experience and the simple luck that had sustained him for years. When the Universe finally saw fit to put him down, he would be moving forward to meet it.

He drew both his pistols, covering either direction.

Time to go to work.

"SWAT! SWAT!" Bolan bellowed. "They're everywhere! Blow the mines!" He pointed his Desert Eagle around the corner and pumped several rounds into the concealed doorway. The .44 Magnum hand cannon was deafening in the enclosed space.

The shouts of alarm from within the judge's chambers were cut short by the splintering of wood and the scream of hot metal shrapnel. The claymore at the doorway had been triggered, shattering the barrier itself. Bolan's ears began ringing from the concussion, but as with so many things, he would simply have to endure it. It was, he knew, nothing short of a miracle that he didn't suffer significant and permanent hearing loss after so many years of firefights.

He thrust his pistols back in their holsters and brought up the M-4, charging the smoking crater where the chambers door had been. Blood stained the ragged opening and coated the floor beyond; the claymore had caught at least one of the terrorists inside. Bolan triggered a short burst of 5.56 mm rounds before vaulting through the doorway.

He almost took a bayonet in the face.

As he entered the room, his senses registered a flash picture of the terrain he faced. The judge's desk was flanked by heavy upholstered chairs, one of which had been overturned. The desk itself was pocked from shrapnel, and everything on top had been shredded. Opposite this were smaller chairs, obviously intended for guests conferring in chambers. They had been knocked over and one was split in two, near the body of the sentry whose blood decorated the blown door. Another corpse was lying, broken and still, near what

Bolan knew was the entrance to the courtroom. This door was bolted from within.

The Executioner processed all of this in an instant, from long habit. As the AK bayonet—a heavy, clip-point blade, like a sturdy bowie knife—sliced through the air toward his eyes, he brought up the barrel of the M-4 and sidestepped. He was able to catch and guide the blade around and to the side, ducking it neatly, placing himself on the outside of the knifer's swing. Bolan immediately reversed his weapon and slammed the retractable butt into the bridge of the attacker's nose.

The neo-Nazi was wild-eyed and bleeding from several deep gouges in his scalp and neck. The neck wound pulsed. The sentry was dying on his feet but didn't know it. Pale with shock and blood loss, he screamed as he tried for another blind, overhand stab. There was no technique here; there was only desperation and rage.

Bolan didn't try to meet the knife. He sidestepped again, crossing the opponent's body, moving out of range. As he went, he brought up his opposite leg in a soccer-style kick. The sole of his combat boot crushed the neo-Nazi's knee joint and the man collapsed, screaming.

The soldier let his rifle fall to the end of its sling. He grabbed the attacker's knife arm, twisted, and torqued the man to the left, tying him up. In the same fluid motion he drove the captured arm in and down.

The bayonet buried itself in the neo-Nazi's stomach.

Bolan dropped to one knee as he shoved in the blade, using his enemy's arm as a lever. His eyes locked with the terrorist's.

"You bastard…" the man said.

"'And then some,'" Bolan told him, ripping the knife across the neo-Nazi's gut. Blood splashed from his abdomen as it erupted from his mouth. Bolan finished him with a tight elbow across the face, snapping his head back, knocking him flat.

Covered in gore, the soldier pushed himself to his feet and sprinted to the courtroom door. Screams and shouts came from the other side. Some were those of hostages, voicing their fear. Others were the terrorists, throwing confused orders to one another, terrified that the moment had come and the police outside were storming the building.

That's when Bolan heard the chopper.

"Sarge!" Grimaldi's voice sounded in his earbud transceiver. "We've got a problem!"

"Jack?" Bolan asked. "Is that you?"

"Negative, Sarge, negative," Grimaldi responded. "The locals have—"

The hollow, metallic clatter of Kalashnikovs on full automatic cut off Grimaldi's words. The commotion had drawn more of the sentries. Evidently Bolan's trick with the mines hadn't caught them all, nor had he realistically expected it would.

They came on without caution, without a plan, without apparent fear. Bolan raised the M-4 and ripped off several measured bursts, meeting the charge. Several of the neo-Nazis who attempted to breach the judge's chambers were already bloody. They might have caught shrapnel from the claymores or simply have been nearby when their comrades did. The suicidal charge they now mounted was a symptom of Bolan's turnabout. He had transformed the predators into prey, so swiftly and unexpectedly that they had reacted with ferocity.

Bolan shot out one man's knees, dropping him to the floor, then pumped a burst of fire into the chest of the next terrorist. Two more gunners appeared hard on the heels of their comrades, and Bolan drilled each in the head with well-placed fire as he aimed through his carbine's optics.

"Say again, Jack, say again," Bolan said. He didn't have

time to hear Grimaldi's reply before the courtroom door behind him was thrown open. The gunmen leaning through the opening held micro-Uzi submachine guns.

Bolan hit the deck.

The swarm of 9 mm rounds scorched the air where he had been standing. With nowhere to go, the soldier rolled sideways, out of the line of fire, until he slammed into the shrapnel-riddled wooden desk. He almost didn't fit with his web gear, but he managed to shove himself under it and through to the other side.

The gunmen were on the move now, pushing into the room and looking for a better angle. They immediately lined up the desk and started firing on it. The heavy oak, which had already suffered extensively, groaned under the onslaught. A round tore the floor near Bolan's left boot. Another burned a furrow in his calf, lightly grazing him. His teeth clenched as the pain bore into him.

Under the gunfire and the ever-louder sound of the chopper, he could feel vibrations in the floor. Footsteps—a lot of them. The occupants of the courtroom were being moved. The helicopter overhead sounded as if it was practically on top of the roof…which it would be, if it were to serve as Nitzche's means of escape.

"—something screwed up out here, Sarge," Grimaldi's voice said into his ear, dotted with static and almost drowned out by the nearby gunfire.

"I need an ID on that chopper!" Bolan shouted. "Jack, intercept! Intercept!"

The desk stopped shaking for a moment.

A grenade skittered across the floor and brushed Bolan's boot.

He would never clear the desk and get beyond the blast radius in time. Instead, Bolan stretched for all he was worth, wrenching something in his shoulder. His fingers found the bomb and he whipped his arm up at the elbow, tossing the deadly steel egg over the desk and back at his attackers.

The explosion had enough force to shove the desk against the wall, pinning him under it. His ears, already ringing, were rattled by the blast. He bit his lip and tasted the coppery tang of blood.

"Sarge, do you read me?" Grimaldi was saying. "Sarge! The locals are telling me to hold at a one-mile perimeter. They've got some FBI hostage negotiator on-site who's cleared a cargo chopper for the terrorists."

"That wasn't the play," Bolan said. He checked his M-4 while crouched under the desk. "Who cleared that?"

"I can't get confirmation," Grimaldi said. "Sarge, you want me to take out the chopper?"

"Who's flying it?"

"No official word," the pilot replied, "but my guess would be either law enforcement or civilian volunteers."

"Innocents, in other words."

"Yeah."

Bolan swore under his breath. "Break the airspace cordon. Block that chopper. Threaten to shoot it down if you have to, but don't fire on it. We've got to cut off Nitzche's escape route."

"You got it, Sarge."

On his back, Bolan got his legs under the desk, then heaved, shoving the heavy piece of furniture across the floor. He wasted no time as he used the desk to cover his move back to his feet. He moved toward the doorway to the courthouse, the M-4 leading the way.

He met no resistance, which told him the courthouse had already been emptied. When Bolan began the dive to the doorway, he went low, extending his arms to keep the M-4 in firing position as he landed painfully on his stomach.

At the last minute he pushed right and slammed into the

wall next to the door. He'd caught a glimpse of another re-mote claymore mine sitting in the opening, a trap set by the gunmen he'd taken down. They had fought a delaying action, giving their leader and his hostages time to get to the roof, and they had left a little explosive package behind just to be sure.

Bolan got to his feet and raced back to the entrance oppo-site the formerly concealed door. Using the wall as cover, he aimed around the corner and simply shot the mine.

The explosion rocked the room, decimating the books and knickknacks on the shelves in the judge's chambers. The smoke was still swirling as Bolan burst through it.

The court was a shambles. The explosion at the chambers' door had done only minor damage, but the terrorists had trashed the place while waiting with the hostages. Whatever wasn't nailed down had been turned over and even shredded. Law books and court records were strewed everywhere. The American flag had been torn to rags, its pole thrust through the seal on the wall behind the judge's bench.

There were several bodies.

A couple were bailiffs, their guns missing from their hol-sters. One had been shot. The other had been stabbed repeat-edly by someone who obviously enjoyed his work.

No one opposed Bolan. The courtroom was empty. The entire building vibrated under the buffeting of the helicop-ter overhead, which would be only a couple yards above his position right now. He felt it as much as heard it.

More mines had been stashed in the stairwell leading up to the balcony, but this time the soldier was ready for them. He skirted the stairs on one side until the steps were chest height, then lifted himself up over the railing, well out of the effective kill zone of the explosives. He hit the stone steps and climbed them two at a time. The balcony was clear of weap-onry. A set of double doors took him to a small anteroom.

The sentry stationed within was pressed against the wall

opposite the door. As he leveled his sawed-off shotgun, Bolan swiveled, bringing up the M-4.

The shotgun roared, the impact slamming into Bolan's gut like a hammer blow. Air rushed from his lungs, and he went down, landing on his back, hard.

The gunman was standing between Bolan and the ladder to the roof. Behind the shotgunner's head, the soldier could see the metal hatch. It was closed.

Then all he could see was the barrel of the shotgun. The neo-Nazi racked the pump action.

"Bye-bye, asshole."

3

Black spots swam in Bolan's vision. He ignored the pain, ignored the burning in his chest, ignored his inability to take in air. Instead, he snapped his feet out and together, creating a scissors that collided with the shotgunner's lead ankle.

Bone snapped.

The gunner screamed and folded, collapsing to one knee as the stark white bone of a compound fracture jutted through the flesh of his leg and a rip in his pant leg. Bolan pushed himself to a sitting position, grabbed the butt of his combat dagger, yanked it free of its scabbard and rammed the curved tip through the neo-Nazi's neck. The blade penetrated up and through, lodging inside his skull, killing him.

Bolan could still hear the helicopter, which was practically on top of him, over the courthouse roof. Just beyond that closed hatch.

"G-Force to Striker!" His transceiver sounded again. "Sarge, we have a big problem here. Washington Metro has scrambled a D.C. MPD chopper to protect the cargo helicopter they're bringing in for the evacuation. The MPD is blocking me. Repeat, Sarge, the Metropolitan Police Department is protecting the cargo chopper! It's a Boeing Model 234 Long Range. If the authorities let them fly loose, they could be six hundred miles away before they need to refuel!"

Bolan tried to speak, but his breath caught in his throat.

He focused on short, shallow breaths. The tension was bad, but he thought it was starting to ease.

He focused on his body, lying very still. Carefully, he moved his hands to his stomach, probing. He found his canvas war bag instead. The fabric was shredded. Magazines and other pieces of equipment were spilling out.

Sitting up, Bolan assessed the damage. Every breath still felt like fire, but they were coming more easily now. A double O buckshot pellet spilled out of his war bag, followed by another. He realized then what had happened. As his body had turned, the sturdy canvas war bag had shifted in front of him. The heavy shot had punched him with all the force of the close-range blast, but the gear in the bag had absorbed some of its energy. The result was a badly bruised abdomen for Bolan—and some items dented and destroyed—but no serious damage that he could detect. With some difficulty he pulled the long, wide strap free from around his neck and over his shoulder. The canvas bag would keep.

Pushing to his hands and knees, he dragged himself to the dead sentry, gripped the hilt of his knife with one hand and pushed against the dead man's forehead with the other. The blade finally came free. Bolan wiped it against the man's battle dress uniform before resheathing it.

He hit the steps of the ladder and grunted as ripples of pain rushed through him. He would be feeling that close call for a while. It didn't matter now; he had no time to worry.

Shoving the hatch open with his shoulder, Bolan risked a look.

Bullets tore into the roof to either side of him. He let himself fall, crashing heavily to the floor below, slowing his descent only by gripping the ladder's uprights with his knees as he slid down. Catching his shoulder at an imperfect angle, he cracked his head and swore as his teeth rattled.

The gunners above ripped the hatch up and chased him

with automatic fire from their micro-Uzis. The opening hatch admitted a small tornado of wind churned up by the cargo helicopter. The neo-Nazis were visible briefly in silhouette against the sky. There were no hostages nearby.

Rolling to dodge the bullets, Bolan yanked a grenade from his web gear, jerked out the pin and counted. The neo-Nazis were just moving to close the access hatch when, as if thrusting a shot put in the Olympics, the Executioner heaved his grenade through the opening. He continued his roll as the explosion rattled the metal hatch in its frame, buckling it. Plaster dust and fragments of concrete pelted his arms while he covered his head from the debris.

"Jack," said Bolan, his ears ringing. "G-Force, come in."

There was no response.

He reached up and touched his ear. The earbud transceiver was gone. It had to have been dislodged during his fall. If Grimaldi was still speaking to him, Bolan's hearing was too far gone at the moment to perceive it.

The only option was the ladder, then the roof. Grimaldi would have to look after things in the air as best he could; there was no way for the soldier to ask for help or suggest options.

The noise of the chopper above was changing pitch, growing more powerful. The craft was lifting off.

Bolan hit the ladder, pausing when the steel structure creaked and groaned, obviously loosened in its mounts by the explosion. The soldier kept going, again putting his shoulder against the hatch, this time straining with all his might against the bent, hot metal. He finally succeeded in dislodging the cover, and pushed through, hitting the roof of the courthouse amid the gritty windstorm that was the big helicopter's rotor wash.

The chopper was hovering three feet off the roof, its doors open. When the neo-Nazis saw Bolan and, more importantly, his modified M-4 carbine, they opened up on him from the chopper with their Kalashnikovs. The soldier took cover behind the only object close enough and strong enough to save him: a large external air-conditioning unit squatting on the rooftop.

The frame of the air conditioner rattled and banged as the 7.62 mm rounds started to smash it apart. Bolan arranged himself to present as compact a target as he could. Then he pressed up with one leg, waited for a lull in the gunfire, and popped up, triggering a blast from his carbine.

He targeted the chopper's rotor. The pilot recognized the threat immediately and began to veer away. It was unlikely Bolan could bring the bird down that way—nor was he putting the hostages in any danger—but if he damaged the rotor sufficiently, any sane pilot would put the aircraft down. There was an equal chance the helicopter would simply fly away to escape the danger. Either way, the hostages would be out of the direct vicinity of the firefight, if only because the neo-Nazis had left their opponent behind.

Where was Grimaldi?

Bolan popped up again and unleashed another blast. The chopper moved farther from the roof, nearing the edge.

Three men jumped out.

The camouflage-clad neo-Nazis ran straight for Bolan's position, firing their weapons. The soldier was impressed; it was the play they were least likely to make, requiring the most guts. He let them blaze away. They were well-trained for their kind, but not compared to him. They didn't stagger their fire, and ran dry on top of one another, scrambling to change magazines. With no choice but to fight or die, they rushed Bolan, perhaps thinking to bludgeon him with the heavy wooden stocks of their assault rifles.

Behind them, the chopper lifted clear and kept going.

Bolan rounded the chewed-up air conditioner and emptied the magazine of his carbine into the first man. He let the weapon fall to the end of its sling, drawing his Beretta 93-R and Desert Eagle in one smooth motion. The men were coming straight for him as his pistols came up, tracking them both.

The Executioner could hit whatever he could see, but he was human.

There simply wasn't time to shoot the men before they collided with him. Bolan hit the roof on his back, tucking his head this time, clenching his jaw against the pain as the neo-Nazis bore him down and crushed him. The shotgun blast to the abdomen made itself known again, as his stomach screamed in pain under the pressure of his two foes.

Bolan slammed the Desert Eagle into the side of the closest man's head and pulled the trigger, punching a round into the roof of the courthouse. The thunder of the pistol against the neo-Nazi's skull burst his eardrum. Screaming, bleeding from the ear, he clapped his hand to the wound, losing his grip on Bolan.

The soldier wrenched his Beretta back on target from beneath the second enemy. He slammed the butt of the Desert Eagle into the man's face and pulled the Beretta's trigger a heartbeat after. His opponent jerked, his eyes rolled up and he collapsed, now nothing but deadweight.

Bolan's hearing was, despite the firefight, returning to normal. The sound of sirens was becoming louder. There were many of them.

Standing, the Executioner stepped in and threw a savage kick into the ribs of the writhing, half-deafened neo-Nazi, who was struggling to draw a pistol from a holster on his hip. The kick caused the terrorist to double up. Bolan bent and, realizing he had nothing with which to secure the man's hands, rolled him over and grabbed him by the collar. He dragged the bleeding, stunned man behind him toward the open hatch and threw him in. The terrorist landed with a crunch as Bolan followed, sliding down the ladder before it came completely free from its frame. Loose now, it rattled within the widened metal collar framing the hatchway.

"Sarge!" a tinny voice was saying from somewhere in the anteroom. "Sarge! Come in!"

Bolan looked toward the neo-Nazi, who was curled in a ball on the floor, and then scanned the space. He spotted his transceiver and snatched it up, replacing it in his ear.

"Sarge!" Grimaldi called once more. "I've lost the chopper, repeat, I have lost the chopper!"

"Striker to G-Force," Bolan said. "Report."

"Sarge, the MPD shielded the helicopter with their own units. They dared me to shoot them down, knowing I wouldn't. Barb and Hal are burning up the airwaves with the powers that be in D.C., but they're stonewalling us. I repeat, they're stonewalling *us*."

Bolan grunted. "No small feat."

"No, it isn't, Sarge," Grimaldi said. "There's more bad news."

"Go ahead."

"Your position is about to be overrun. Police, fire, first re-sponse medical… It's a zoo out there now that Nitzche and his men have pulled out."

"Understood," Bolan said. He began rummaging through the shredded remains of his canvas bag, sorting out the un-damaged equipment and munitions from the rest. He found several of his plastic zip-tie cuffs and used these to secure the deafened terrorist's wrists and ankles.

In the little time he had left, the soldier redistributed ev-erything he could from the ruined war bag to his web. Fortu-nately, most of his loaded magazines had survived the assault. A few pieces of electronic and countermeasures gear were destroyed. Finally, he found the item that had saved his life: a slim netbook computer, sheathed in a Kevlar skin designed by

John "Cowboy" Kissinger. The tiny computer was wrecked, bent into a V-shape from the fist-size punch of heavy shot at close range. It was the point of that V that had bruised Bolan's gut, as brutal as any spear-hand blow to naked flesh.

He heard footsteps echoing from the courtroom beyond the anteroom. His company was here.

"Freeze!" someone shouted.

"Don't move!" another man roared.

Bolan was suddenly very aware of the many rifles and shotguns pointed at him.

"We have him," shouted one of the members of the Special Response Team. They were wearing Kevlar helmets and body armor and wielded MP-5 machine pistols.

"Federal agent," Bolan said, standing and holding his arms out at chest height, palms open.

"He's armed for bear, sir," one of the SRT operatives said.

"I can see that."

"Cooper," Bolan said. "Matthew Cooper. Justice Department. My credentials are in my pocket."

"Let's see them, Cooper," the first man said. His subdued name tag read Reynolds.

The soldier produced his identification, provided for him by Stony Man Farm. He offered it to Reynolds and was very careful to make no moves that could be construed as hostile. His weapons were all in position about his body, the M-4 at the end of its sling. The SRT team was as aware of this as Bolan was.

The neo-Nazi on the floor moaned. One of the SRT men jerked an MP-5 on track to cover him.

"Who's that?" Reynolds demanded.

"One of Nitzsche's men," Bolan said.

When the SRT men looked at each other, he added, "One of the terrorists."

Another contingent of armed, armored SRT personnel arrived at the entrance to the anteroom. The lead man's tag read Reed.

"Sir," Reed said. He spared Bolan a wary glance. "The building is cleared. We have emergency personnel on-site and sweeping the building for stragglers."

"There are men on the roof," Bolan said.

"Active hostiles?" Reynolds asked.

"Neutralized," Bolan replied. "Like him." He jerked his chin to the terrorist on the floor.

"What'd you do to him?" Reed asked, bending to check the fallen man. "His ear is gushing blood."

"He wouldn't listen," Bolan said.

Reynolds eyed the Executioner disapprovingly. He handed over the identification. "So *you're* the one."

"Sir?" Reed asked.

"His people at Justice have been jerking my chain all morning," Reynolds said. "They aren't happy about the decision to let the chopper through. Seems Captain Go-It-Alone here has an attack chopper up there whose pilot doesn't listen to local authority very well. Maybe he's hard of hearing, too, Cooper?"

"I was told I would have full authority," Bolan said. "Your men let the terrorists escape with live hostages. My air support and I could have prevented that."

"We all answer to somebody, Cooper," Reynolds said. "My orders come from the top of the chain here in D.C."

"I doubt that," Bolan said.

"To go higher you'd have to go to the President, tough guy," Reynolds stated. When Bolan didn't blink at that, he looked less sure of himself. "Had you interfered, they might have started killing hostages."

"Had we cut off their escape," Bolan said, "killing hostages wouldn't have done them any good. They'd have traded their own lives for the lives of the captives."

"I guess we'll never know," Reynolds said. "Whatever authority you think you have, Cooper, I'm not interested. Nitzche is gone, and so is your reason to be here. Get out of my crime scene."

Bolan turned to leave. He paused when Reed looked up. "Strange," the SRT man said.

"What?" Reynolds asked.

"I wouldn't have pegged them for the suicide type," Reed said, searching the pockets of the terrorist's camouflage fatigues. "That's not really the profile of..." He stopped. "Hey. What's this?"

Reed had lifted the hem of the terrorist's BDU blouse, probably to check for weapons at the waistline. The terrorist was wearing another uniform shirt underneath the fatigues. Reed ripped the BDU open, popping buttons. The logo on the chest of the uniform shirt was unmistakable.

"DCFD," Reynolds said. The terrorist was dressed as a District of Columbia Firefighter.

"Oh, shit..." Reed said.

Bolan was on the move before the SRT men could think to stop him.

Of course the neo-Nazis weren't ready to give up their lives. It wasn't their style; it wasn't how they did things. If Nitzche had left men behind to cover his escape, he would have provided for them a plausible means of escape. It wouldn't matter to him if the escape plan actually worked or not. It only had to seem workable to the men staying behind in the courthouse.

It was possible the shooters from the chopper had planned to exit the helicopter at the last moment regardless of resistance offered. That made sense: ensure Nitzche's escape, then remain behind to counter any last-minute resistance by the locals.

It also made sense that there would be one or two terrorists hiding somewhere in the building to serve as a rear guard. They would have waited for the worst of the battle to pass them by, then blended with the inevitable mop-up chaos— simply by shedding their paramilitary uniforms.

Taking the steps two and three at a time, Bolan ran past startled emergency personnel working their way through the corridors. He hit the street, and the crush of vehicles and bystanders, at a dead run.

Someone screamed.

Bolan looked left, then right. He spotted the fire department vehicles, and then, in the opposite direction, a pair of men dressed as DCFD.

"Federal agent!" Bolan yelled. "Down!"

He brought his carbine to his shoulder and fired.

4

Klaus Nitzche prepared his carved ivory pipe, brought for him from his estate in Argentina. The tobacco provided to him wasn't his favorite blend, but it was tolerable. Anything was better than the cheap, often stale cigarettes with which he had been forced to make do while in prison.

He was cold. Even with the large door shut, and even with his heavy overcoat draped around his shoulders like a cape, the cold seeped into his old bones and made him shiver. It had been cold in his holding cell, too.

It galled him that he still wore the orange jumpsuit in which he had been brought to trial. To deny him the opportunity to face his accusers dressed as a man, to force him to look the part of the criminal before his trial had even begun... these were only some of the many petty insults he had been forced to endure.

Nitzche was a proud man. He had reason to be. From an early age, he had understood that the key to greatness was pride. If a person believed in himself, if he knew himself to be better than others, those beliefs became self-fulfilling prophecies. They drove a man, forced him to be better than his enemies, better than his competitors. They became the measure of what he was. They became everything.

If it was true for a man, it was true for a nation.

He remembered vividly the awful day he'd realized that

his nation, his Germany, had no pride. His father was dead, a victim of overwork and a weak heart. Klaus had tried to speak with his mother about it. She was a whipped dog, content to keep her nose down and her standards low. She didn't understand. She couldn't help him.

Germany was crippled by war and economic ruin. Its people had the mind-set of the defeated. Its people had lost their pride.

And then everything changed.

Nitzche fussed over the pipe, packing it just so. His fingers trembled. Arthritis threatened to turn his hands into claws. He *willed* them to work. He wouldn't be laid low by something as insignificant as sickness. Sickness was of the body, and the body answered to the mind.

Klaus Nitzche's mind was superior.

From the first rays of hope that were the Führer's ascendancy to power, Nitzche had known things would be different. He had nothing but hate for those who refused to support Hitler willingly. It was obvious from the outset that Hitler offered Germany everything she had lost: power, respect, position. And something so much more important than the rest: the pride that accompanied these other things, these lesser things.

Indio, faithful Indio, leaned over from his seat and snapped open the chrome pipe lighter he always carried. The enormous Uruguayan had been, in his younger days, a Tupamaro—one of Uruguay's leftist guerrillas, styled after a legendary Incan leader who once fought a revolution against the Spanish conquistadores. He carried a seemingly endless supply of knives and bore the scars of many a blade fight. The most notable of these was the oldest—a wide runnel marking his forehead, cheek and left eye socket. The socket held a black glass orb Indio affected for its menace. Around his neck, he wore a necklace of six brass rifle shells, which he claimed were the first six shots he had ever fired as a Tupamaro. On his hip the South American giant carried a well-worn Tokarev pistol, which also dated to his revolutionary days.

As Nitzche puffed contentedly on his pipe despite the chill, he chuckled to himself. The thought of one like Indio in his employ, much less as a trusted lieutenant and field commander, would have horrified him as a younger man. He had been so full of idealism at that age. So eager to prove that the Führer and his notions of purity were true to the letter of Aryan law.

Yet those ideas of purity, those assertions to perfection, hadn't saved Hitler and those closest to him. In the end, even the Führer's pride had failed him. In the end, he had embraced defeat, reportedly taking his own life rather than be captured by the enemy. Such a waste. Such a tremendous disappointment.

When the time came for Nitzche to abandon Schlechterwald, as the enemy advanced on the camp, it had been the simplest of matters to marshal the men loyal to him and implement the contingency plans he had put in place. A wise military leader always allowed for the possibility of failure. To do otherwise was, well, it could be called prideful, but Nitzche knew there was a line between pride and hubris that could not be crossed. The latter led one to make foolish mistakes, such as holing up in a bunker and refusing to admit that the war was lost, and some other means of continuing the fight had to be found.

Working his way up in the wartime German hierarchy hadn't been difficult. Nitzche was intelligent, ruthless and enthusiastic. Most importantly, he got results, ringing every possible ounce of blood and sweat from Schlechterwald's forced labor ranks. With the war well under way, Nitzche's tendency to get results had saved him from the wrath of his superiors when he'd decided to take leadership of the camp more directly in hand. He had, through the years, even managed to forget the name of the SS officer he had killed in order to take over his job.

Yet he remembered vividly what it had felt like to squeeze the life from the man's throat. He had grabbed the fool by the neck, placed his thumbs oh so precisely and pressed, squeezed, clenched for all he was worth. The flush brought to the SS commander's face had been so great that Nitzche could feel the heat radiating from the man's cheeks. The sound that had escaped the dead man's lips, when Nitzche had finally released him, was like nothing he had known before or since.

The things one forgot weren't strange at all, considering. One remembered the important details. One discarded the irrelevancies.

He remembered, for example, the day that Indio had joined his employ. In the period immediately before and after the fall of the Third Reich, many refugees from the Nazi regime had fled to Argentina and its somewhat sympathetic commercial and political climates.

Nitzche was no refugee.

Power over a camp like Schlechterwald was power over a means of production, over a lot of resources and their distribution. Nitzche had used his power to divert funds and supplies to his contingency plan. As the war effort grew more dire, and Germany's chances less certain, he had accelerated his own planning. Were his beloved country to know another military defeat at Hitler's hands and on Hitler's watch, Nitzche would nonetheless continue on in the spirit of the Führer's best teachings.

So when he was forced to withdraw from Schlechterwald with his private forces, the loyalty of which he had cultivated through long familiarity—and more than a few bribes— Nitzche traveled to Argentina not as a fleeing refugee, but as a determined soldier.

Through the years he'd focused on building his organization. That was made both easier and harder by the fact that Heil Nitzche had no clearly defined goal. Klaus followed global politics keenly and watched as other political and terrorist movements waxed and waned. He followed the social protest movements, too. Without exception they were unfocused, poorly led and ineffectual, even when abundantly funded and resourced.

Over the years, his perspective on the superiority of the Aryan race also evolved.

Yes, it was true that those of Aryan descent were superior, but that was no longer a guiding philosophy in and of itself. It simply couldn't be. Were innate superiority all that mattered, Hitler couldn't have lost to the coalition of race-mixing inferiors who'd stood against him.

In time Nitzche had come to liken the idea to a pack of wild dogs. In every pack there were stronger dogs and weaker ones. The latter deferred to the former, but the pack worked toward common goals.

It would be foolish for Nitzche, as the leader of his own pack, to discard a specific powerful, fearsome dog simply because he judged that dog's breed inferior. And while ultimately the pack might operate toward some idealistic goal—in Nitzche's case, the overall ideal of Aryan supremacy represented by political power in Nitzche's hands—every pack's more immediate purpose was the protection and furtherance of itself.

Nitzche and HN had therefore built an organization whose purpose was simply to strengthen Nitzche and his men. This focus on strength for its own sake had allowed HN, and its many resources, to remain below the radar of the many counterterrorist units that operated around the globe.

It was also that focus of strength as the end goal that had brought to Nitzche's banner a variety of men who might never have sought his protection otherwise. He was currently alone among those of his contingent who had traveled to Argentina from the collapsing Third Reich. He had outlived them all. That was just as well, for many of the neo-Nazi soldiers Nitzche now cultivated would have caused his old supporters more than slight pause.

He had begun recruiting from many light-skinned races of color, most extensively those from South America, uniting them as neo-Nazis under the philosophies of national socialism and of might was right. The type of men Nitzche needed to form the ranks of his soldiers—simple, ruthless, obedient, but vicious—responded well to his modified approach. In showing them kindness, in lavishing on them resources and even gifts, in showing them that he valued their devotion to him, he succeeded in creating a cult of personality. Heil Nitzche wasn't just a neo-Nazi organization. It was an organization devoted to Nitzche first and foremost.

Indio passed him a thermos of coffee. From the taste, Nitzche knew it to be decaf, but in truth, his doctors had forbade him anything stronger. Still, the gesture mattered, and he patted the enormous man on one rock-hard shoulder, smiling and nodding. Nitzche sipped the coffee, enjoying the warmth if not the flavor.

Indio had been close to death, that day in the alley behind a decrepit bar in Buenos Aires. Nitzche and his convoy had been passing through, taking the side streets as they customarily did, when Nitzche ordered his driver to stop. There, inspiring in his indomitable will, Indio fought no less than eight men, all of them armed with pipes, bricks or knives. They had bloodied the giant, but Indio's opponents couldn't break him, even as they swarmed him from every side and dragged him to the bloody pavement.

How perfect a metaphor for Germany's own defeat! Nitzche could see in Indio's fierce determination shades of the nation he had been forced to leave behind. His brown skin might mark him as inferior, but Indio was a worthy dog none-theless. Nitzche had ordered his men to wade into the battle. They had reduced the odds until Indio could fight back, then stood aside at Nitzche's orders. The giant had smashed his enemies with renewed energy, then turned and bowed to his new benefactor. He had been Nitzche's most ardent supporter ever since, paying lip service to his neo-Nazi philosophies, while clearly interested only in protecting Nitzche himself.

Indio's only other interest was rape, Nitzche had to admit. On the streets of Buenos Aires, the local prostitutes knew his name and feared it. No man was without flaws, Nitzche supposed.

The arrangement suited Klaus Nitzche. Fate had smiled on them both. Every one of Nitzche's men secretly hoped that he would be selected to adopt the mantle of leadership after Nitzche's passing. Indio alone made no mention and gave no sign of this ambition. He was content merely to serve, his personal honor wrapped up in the debt he believed he owed the much older man. In truth, it didn't matter to Nitzche who assumed leadership when he was gone, or even if Heil Nitzche survived. It existed to serve and protect him, and after his death, what happened to its members mattered to him not at all.

Indio wore a headset, as did several of the men, so they could communicate despite the noise of the helicopter. He offered one to Nitzche, then helped him put it on his head as Nitzche continued to smoke his pipe.

"Yes, Indio?" the old man asked.

"My leader, the pilot reports there is no sign of pursuit." Indio's command of English was superb. He hadn't spoken a word of it until Nitzche asked that he learn. English served as the language in common among all his recruits, because many of them spoke it. Since the death of the last of his origi-nal lieutenants, Nitzche hadn't had occasion to speak German to any of his supporters. The emotion this thought brought him might have been regret, but on the whole, Nitzche wasn't sentimental. He cared only to be as strong as he could be and to make those who had hurt him pay.

"That is excellent," he said. "And not unexpected."

"How did you know, sir?" Indio rumbled. He had the deepest voice of any man Klaus had ever encountered. "How could you be certain the authorities wouldn't simply pluck us from the sky, force us down?"

"For the same reason that I should have anticipated the interference of that wretched bounty hunter," Nitzche said, spitting the last two words. "On whose shoulders rest the blame for this entire miserable affair."

"The Berwalds?" Indio asked.

"The very same." He nodded. "No one among the Jewish Nazi-hunters has more tenacity than Berwald, except perhaps his bastard son." Klaus paused to take a long puff from his pipe. "And who among our enemies, who have for so many years rooted out our fellows, would have the political clout to make sure the police didn't simply shoot us down or somehow make us land? I sense the Berwalds know that, free of the fools who would jail me, I will not be caught twice."

"They wish you free…." Indio began.

"Yes," Nitzche said. "They wish me free so they may deal with me themselves. They will not trust the courts to do it a second time. We have amassed as much information about the Nazi-hunter groups as they have amassed about us. We knew almost everything there was to know about Lantern before they ever had me in their clutches. Doubtless I have few secrets from them, either. That is how they knew where to send the bounty hunter to take me. How goes that operation, incidentally?"

"Our men in Hawaii are closing in," Indio said.

"I want him killed," Nitzche stated, nodding, "but slowly.

Make him suffer. Record it, so that we may distribute the video online. I wish it known what happens to all who presume to make a fool of Klaus Nitzche."

"Of course, sir," Indio said. "My leader, I have taken the opportunity of…disciplining the men assigned to guard you the day the bounty hunter captured you. Had they followed protocol, they would never have been separated from you."

"Such," Nitzche said, "is the price of one's appetites." The old man had, in fact, been visiting Buenos Aires's most exclusive brothel the day the bounty hunter captured him. Nitzche had grown somewhat complacent in his later years, making a habit of visiting the establishment every Sunday. This practice had no doubt become known to Lantern's intelligence network. He'd made such trips with minimal guard for the sake of discretion, something he would know better than to indulge in again.

Nitzche knew, too, that Indio's idea of "discipline" was to gouge out a man's eyes with his knife before killing him. It was one of the things that made his assistant so valuable. A fit of rage on the big man's part made it possible to extract the harshest penalty for failure, while maintaining the fiction that he cared deeply for all his men and would never treat them so harshly. What was it that old Italian had said? "It is better to be feared than loved when one of the two must be lacking." Yes, it was something like that.

Nitzche understood the value of creating both emotions in his followers.

Feeling his belly full at last, he handed the thermos back to Indio and gestured with his pipe. The rear portion of the large transport helicopter was full of the kneeling hostages and their armed guards. Among those Nitzche had captured was the judge, one Amy Ballard. She was a gray-haired, severe woman with a matronly demeanor and a miserable tongue. During his preliminary appearances before the court, she had grandstanded from the bench more than once, expressing her contempt for Klaus Nitzche and everything she believed he stood for.

Also present were the court reporter—a fairly attractive young woman—and a handful of other court functionaries and spectators. The prosecutor, an older man named Lars Kinsey, was there, as was Nitzche's own sniveling court-appointed defense counsel, Kevin Orwin. There were also two bailiffs. Their weapons had been taken from them.

"Have you heard from the men we stationed to cover our departure?" Nitzche asked.

"No, sir," Indio said. "There has been no call. Each man had a prepaid wireless phone, but they may have fallen to the operative in black."

"That wouldn't explain why the men stationed in the courthouse itself also fail to report," Nitzche said. "But no matter. There are two court guards among the hostages."

"Yes, my leader," Indio said.

"Bring them to me. Separately."

"Yes, my leader." Indio produced a shoe box from under his crash seat and opened it. Inside, swathed in a soft cloth, was a beautifully maintained presentation-grade Luger pistol. As Nitzche watched, Indio checked the magazine and chambered a round, operating the toggle action. He reversed the burnished, heavily engraved weapon and handed it over almost reverently, bowing his head.

Nitzche felt the grip of the familiar weapon fill his hand. The sensation of the steel and wood against his palm chased away the pain of his arthritis.

The first bailiff, sensing what awaited him, began to tremble with fear as he was forced to his knees before the old Nazi.

Smiling, Klaus Nitzche pointed the barrel of the Luger between the man's eyes and, without a word, pulled the trigger.

5

"They were fit to be tied, Sarge," Grimaldi said. The two conversed through their shared transceiver link.

Bolan, resupplied and with a replacement canvas war bag to haul his extra munitions, was as prepared as he was likely to be. "I don't have any patience for these jurisdictional games," he admitted.

"Neither does Barb or Hal, from the sound of it," Grimaldi told him. "The report should be coming through now, if the relay from the gear up here is working like it should."

"It is," Bolan said. His secure satellite smartphone was vibrating, indicating that intelligence files were once more incoming from Stony Man Farm. He read through them, skimming the reports of communications between Operations at the Farm, Brognola's office, the Justice Department officially, and both Brognola and Price unofficially. The messages painted a pretty bleak picture of the complex halls of power both the Farm's operatives and Brognola, as director of the Sensitive Operations Group, were forced to travel during a given mission.

Authorization for the police interference with Grimaldi's mission had indeed come from highly placed personnel in D.C., though of course not from the very top. It was the top, after all, from which Bolan and the Farm got their orders. A lot of fingers were being pointed, but nobody had stepped forward or thrown anyone else under the bus. All the Farm had right now was conjecture.

That conjecture pointed in each case to Lantern and the Berwalds. The group was known to have plenty of influence in government circles. It was through use of this influence that the illegal extradition—some of the tabloids and all of the racist shortwave and internet radio broadcasts called it "illegal kidnapping"—of Nitzche had been overlooked, so that the old Nazi could be processed through and put on trial in the United States judicial system. Clearly, the Berwalds had called on some bureaucrat or a group of them, planting the idea that to interfere with the chopper would be to signal the death of all aboard. Weaker men and weaker minds had prevailed, resulting in the temporary blocking of Bolan's operation. All this happened regardless of the Farm's presidential authority. Having the ear, and the orders, of the Man wasn't always enough.

The awkwardness of the situation was compounded by the fact that Grimaldi would have blasted his way through just about any opposition—except law enforcement. The cops were, even when working against the Farm in this case, still on their side. Jack Grimaldi would no more pull the trigger on a law-enforcement officer than would Mack Bolan.

When Bolan had drawn down on the two "firemen," it had been a near thing. He had fired into the sidewalk near their feet, seeking to provoke a reaction that would confirm or deny the men's friend-or-foe status. He wasn't disappointed. At the first sign of gunfire both men had dropped and spun, pulling pistols from under their shirts. Bolan had put each of them down, risking getting shot by the locals for his efforts. It wasn't until an official from DCFD confirmed that the pair weren't his men that the SRT and police officers agreed to release the man they thought was "Matthew Cooper."

The operation so far had been fraught with problems.

Bolan didn't like it. Success in combat involved momentum. You had to seize and keep the momentum going to ensure victory. Every complication, every false start, every detention at the hands of the forces that were *supposed* to be helping him robbed him of that momentum. His current journey with Grimaldi was part of the effort to retake the initiative in this small war with Klaus Nitzche. The Farm had arranged a series of refueling stops, using mobile tanker trucks, to help get the pair where they needed to go.

While Grimaldi had been helpless to do anything with police choppers blocking him, the Farm had responded to the pilot's calls for help by using its network of satellite access points. High-resolution imaging from space had enabled them to track Nitzche's chopper to its ultimate destination. The old Nazi had gone to ground in a large tract of privately owned property in rural Kansas.

Thermal imaging of that property had proved interesting. The land was registered to a holding company that Aaron "the Bear" Kurtzman and his cybernetic team at Stony Man Farm had traced to Nitzche's covert network. Staying low-profile as he had, over the years, Nitzche had amassed quite an empire, spanning financial reserves and real property. Quite a bit of that was in Argentina, but the man obviously believed in planning ahead. Heil Nitzche held several properties and business entities in the United States, most likely to serve Nitzche in the event that he was ever brought there—or anywhere in North America, for that matter—for trial. It made sense. Such an eventuality would be something that would weigh heavily on the mind of a war criminal like Nitzche. While the man probably felt no remorse for his crimes, he most certainly would have a healthy aversion to being caught and held accountable for them.

The Farm had produced, and sent to Bolan's phone, an extensive set of maps detailing the tunnel and trench system surrounding the center of the property. The satellite imagery had also determined that Nitzche's safehouse—really a fortified bunker, far from what passed for civilization in that part of Kansas—was protected by antiaircraft weaponry. That meant Bolan would have no choice but to insert at the edge of the property and then sneak, creep and fight his way through the maze of defenses that Nitzche and his very well-manned, well-equipped group had erected. This bunker was, after all, Nitzche's go-to-ground spot; it would be designed to make him feel safe despite whatever threats faced him. Such a bunker was the very definition of a "hard site." It wouldn't be easy to breach.

The rolling grasslands were quite flat, affording Nitzche and his men a very good field of fire. There were, however, variations and hillocks, including a small stand of trees at the far southern edge of the area where Bolan's plans said the bunker trenches began. The grove extended for some distance. Possibly it delineated a property border. Bolan didn't care, as long as he could get in. Grimaldi would have to withdraw to a safe distance, out of range of the bunker's antiaircraft weapons.

Fully equipped and ready, the Executioner hit the grass as the chopper dipped and hooked skyward once more. It paused long enough to throw a salute to Grimaldi before making his way into the small stand of trees. The relative flatness of the terrain, and the distance he could see accordingly, was amazing.

Crouching to present a smaller target, and keenly aware of the possibility of sniper fire from the direction of the bunker, Bolan used his satellite phone to guide him. The device gave him a GPS reference coordinate and would lead him to the outermost tendril of the extensive network of trenches dug into the Kansas soil.

He was on his own from this point. Grimaldi was available for emergencies, but losing the chopper, not to mention one of Bolan's oldest friends, made the prospect of forcing the pilot to dodge anti-aircraft missiles or machine-gun fire a less than attractive prospect.

The leading edge of the trench was flush with the earth and camouflaged by green-and-brown spray paint. The paint had been used to match, roughly, the surrounding grass. Bolan moved in a half crouch as he took the path leading down, impressed by how smoothly and evenly the trench had been dug. Someone, or more probably, a lot of someones, had spent a great deal of time digging these fortifications with precision equipment or a lot of human muscle.

While there was still plenty of light from above, the trench grew darker as it deepened. Bolan removed the combat light from his gear and thumbed it on as he walked. The bright LED beam revealed no sign of tripwires or sensors, although he knew of plenty of means of intrusion detection that would be invisible to the intruder himself. He would never see a buried piezoelectric sensor, for example, but the pressure of his passing would trip the alarm. Even the chopper insertion could have alerted the nest of neo-Nazis to Bolan's presence. He was resigned to the fact that surprise wasn't on his side, or couldn't be for long.

The trench was soon deep enough that it extended about two feet above his head. He could see evidence of wiring strung along the walls, from which common task lights had been hung. These weren't lit. He walked up to one and tried to switch it on, but nothing happened. It either wasn't connected to a functioning power source, or was controlled from somewhere else, possibly the bunker.

Bolan squatted and consulted his phone, shielding the display with his hand. He verified where he was, memorized the layout of the next few passages and put the phone away. He could repeat the process indefinitely if necessary, working his way through the maze of trenches in chunks, until he finally encountered serious resistance.

The hostages, and Nitzche himself, were at the other end of this yellow brick road. It was time to go calling on the Wizard.

Bolan reached a junction where two trenches met two tunnels. The tunnels ran left and right, while the trenches continued on, toward his goal. A small room of sorts had been dug out here. There was quite a bit of space in which to wait or to fight. He was about to move on when something, some sixth combat sense, alerted him.

He wasn't alone.

The soldier felt the oncoming foe before he heard or saw him. The floor of the trench transmitted vibration. He had just enough time to raise his arm before the black-clad opponent crashed into him. Bolan took the impact and swiveled, throwing the attacker over his hip. The dark figure rolled to the floor of the trench.

There were more. They wore black BDUs, and black balaclavas over their faces. They moved inexpertly, or at least the first two did. Bolan managed to throw the second one, pushing him off balance easily. The third one, however, was another matter.

Bolan heard the metallic snick of an expanding baton opening. The weapon whistled through the air above his head a moment later. He ducked, stepped in and threw a short punch that staggered the baton-wielder. Then he turned and stripped the weapon from the man's hand.

Armed with the baton now, Bolan gripped the foam rubber handle and whipped the weapon this way and that. The two men he had thrown were back on their feet and eager for more. He didn't disappoint them.

They hadn't tried to shoot him. They wore holstered sidearms, but hadn't gone for them. That told him they weren't Nitzche's men, who had no compunctions about gunning down anyone. These weren't law-enforcement personnel, either, if Bolan was any judge of their demeanor and their gear.

These could only be Berwald's Lantern operatives.

Lantern was well financed and highly motivated, unafraid of direct action. While their budget was probably dwarfed by Nitzche's own, given that the old Nazi had what amounted to a private army, Lantern was the opposite side of the Heil Nitzche coin. One was good, if misguided; the other was evil. The two were going to collide, with disastrous results, unless Bolan did something about it. These Lantern people had no concept of the meat grinder they were about to drop themselves into.

Bolan allowed the two black-clad foes to dance in and out for a while, testing him. At least they *thought* they were testing him. In reality he was toying with them, selecting the best options for neutralizing them without hurting them too badly. While the Lantern operatives weren't law enforcement and were operating outside the law, he could hardly fault them for the latter on moral grounds. Still, they were relative amateurs from the look of them, and they had no business playing around on turf that would get them hurt or killed. They were little better than a distraction, from that point of view.

The third fighter was up again, and now all three circled Bolan like sharks. Each time they closed the distance with a kick or an out-of-range punch, the soldier whipped them with the tip of the baton, producing several hisses of pain and grunts of discomfort. Finally, Bolan decided he had indulged them enough. They were wasting his time and weren't getting the hint he was trying to give.

Bolan stopped moving.

He stood completely still, the baton held low in front of his body. He rested his left hand on the end of the stick and simply waited.

They thought it was a trick at first, and froze with him.

Finally, the one he had punched, perhaps looking for some payback, took a step in. Bolan watched that step and saw, in the dim light, the man turn his heel inward for a roundhouse kick. Bolan let it come, shifting to meet it at the last instance, slamming the baton across the knee joint. He was far gentler than he could have been.

The man went down, shrieking, holding his knee.

The second fighter came in. Again Bolan held completely still, until the last moment, when he whipped the baton up in a backhand arc. He pulled the blow at the last moment, but still laid the weapon across the man's face.

"You son of a—" began the second fighter thickly. From the sound, his lip was split and bloody, swelling rapidly.

Bolan stepped forward. He raised the baton and swung it at the third man's face, stopping just short of his target.

"Anytime I want to," Bolan said, "I can make you and your friends fall down."

"Kill him!" the second fighter ordered. "Kill him now!"

"Enough!" the third man said. "Shut up!"

He pointed at Bolan. "Who are you?"

"Federal agent," the soldier replied. "Cease and desist. Leave this area now. You have no business here."

"He's lying!" said the man with the sprained knee. "He didn't identify himself before when he could have. He's one of them! He's some kind of scout for Nitzche's forces!"

"If I was with Klaus Nitzche," Bolan said, shaking his head, "I would have shot you all and been on my way long before now."

That silenced them for a time. Finally, the second fighter helped the man with the injured knee to his feet and let him lean on him for support. The two put some space between themselves and Bolan, as if they thought the soldier might lash out and strike them again if they stood too close.

"I told you," Bolan said. "I'm a federal agent, here to free the hostages being held by Klaus Nitzche."

"And then what?" said the third fighter. "Nitzche is allowed to remain at large? Or you'll take him into custody again, so that he can simply break free once more?"

"Exactly what is the alternative?" Bolan asked. "I'm not going to allow him to walk free."

"You should *kill* him!" said the man with the injured knee. It wasn't clear if he was referring to Nitzche or to Bolan. The third man made no attempt to go for his sidearm. Bolan paid careful attention to the other two to make sure neither of them got any ideas.

"I'm out of time," he told them. "We're done playing this game. I'm giving you an opportunity to leave. Call it the lesser of the possible evils. Force me to and I'll take *you* into custody, too, to keep you out of my way until my work here is done."

"Do you have any idea how many kilometers of trench and tunnel are between us and that bunker if we take a wrong turn?" said the third man. "Do you really think you, alone, can make your way to Nitzche's bunker, much less fight past his men?"

"Do you?" Bolan retorted.

"We're done here," the man said. "Go your own way, government man. We'll do the same. Maybe we'll even see each other along the way."

"Not acceptable," Bolan said. His hand shot to the holster behind his hip and he yanked the Desert Eagle free. He brought the big pistol up to cover the third man, the triangular snout of the .44 Magnum pistol centered on the nose of his balaclava. "Now, here's how it's going to be. Back off. Go home. Last chance."

The third man waited through a ten-count before moving or speaking.

"No," he said simply.

Bolan resisted the urge to swear. The Lantern operative had correctly deduced that the big American was going light on these people. He wasn't prepared to shoot them dead, not if they weren't directly threatening his life. However, the Lantern man hadn't considered that Bolan had force alternatives that weren't necessarily fatal.

The other two began to bicker with each other in stage whispers. Bolan would deal with them in turn. He worked the scenario quickly through in his mind.

A smash to the face with the barrel of the Desert Eagle would stun the third man, allowing Bolan to cover the other two and, if absolutely necessary, shoot low if they tried for their guns. He would be as cautious as possible, but—

The footfalls were too close when he finally heard them over the arguing men, and it was then that Bolan knew he had been tricked.

"Don't move or I'll kill you," a new voice said.

The barrel of the gun was cold against the back of his neck.

6

Eli Berwald Jr., "Aaron" to everyone but his mother when she was alive, crouched in the trench and read the laminated map by the filtered red glow of the tactical LED flashlight he carried. He swore when he realized he wasn't sure which path was the shortest. The trenches and tunnels were convoluted, switching back on one another deliberately to form kill zones and fatal funnels.

So far, there had been no sign of Nitzche's forces. For that he was grateful. His people would be forced to fight for their lives soon enough. When that moment came, Berwald wasn't sure how many would stand and fight and how many would cut and run.

It wasn't that they suffered deficits of character. Every member was a person of good stature who stood with Lantern because he or she believed in the ideals of the organization. Still, how could he expect his men and women to become soldiers at the drop of a hat? Most were idealists, patriots. They had the will and, in some cases, the training. But none of them were battle-tested.

This day that would change.

Berwald's father had built a powerful advocacy organization. There was much money to be had in the work of defending Israel and her people from the many who hated her. Despite the countless anti-Semites arrayed against them, and even though many of these forces had powerful lobbies of their own—or perhaps because of it—the elder Berwald had had no trouble making Lantern a lobbying force to be reckoned with. He had begun this work as a young man, upon entering the United States. So profoundly affected was he by his experience in Schlechterwald, and by the loss of his parents there, that Eli Berwald Sr. could think of nothing but ensuring that such a horror never occurred again.

Raising money, and investing that money to make more, had proved easy enough for him. He was even careful to keep all—or most—of what Lantern did with its finances completely legal. They had survived multiple audits by the time Aaron was old enough to come on board, and his dad insisted that this remain the case. When Aaron took over the day to day operations of Lantern, he abided by his father's wishes.

Less simple was the task of getting him to agree to more direct action.

When Aaron had assumed his position, taking from his father's shoulders the responsibility for most of the operational and financial functions of Lantern, they were sitting on vast untapped potential. Under the elder Berwald, Lantern had used its money to influence lawmakers, network with lobbying groups, fund Holocaust remembrance functions and memorials, and hire private investigators to locate stray members of the old Nazi regime. Under Aaron, however, the group took its activities a step further, shaping events rather than simply prodding them into being indirectly.

It was because of him that, rather than just spending money on the detectives to find Klaus Nitzche, they had hired the famous television bounty hunter to go to Argentina to bring him back. There would have been no way to drag Nitzche to justice otherwise; even if an arrangement between the government of the United States and that of Argentina could be reached, the Argentines, whom Nitzche almost certainly would have been bribing extensively, couldn't be trusted to act on it.

Aaron had also begun training his Lantern personnel to fight. That move had been a point a contention between him and his father for some time; Eli the elder, while he lived in fear of a second Holocaust, nonetheless thought making the transition to direct acts of counterviolence was a line that shouldn't be crossed. The two had argued about it for some time. Aaron had eventually won, because he was more persistent, and because he had already implemented the training programs, regardless of his father's wishes. Since that time he had focused on stockpiling weapons and other supplies. If society were to break down, if the veneer of civilization were to be torn away, Lantern and its people wouldn't be taken unaware. Aaron had worried over these concerns of social chaos ever since watching the news reports of Hurricane Katrina, and seeing how quickly society's members devolved into violent animals.

That savagery, that forsaking of the rules and laws that supposedly protected men and women in modern life, had disturbed Aaron deeply. His father accused him of becoming some latter-day apocalyptic Jew, a survivalist. Aaron countered that the work of Lantern had always been the survival of the Jewish people. There was little difference except venue, in his mind, between fighting anti-Israel legislation in Congress by exerting influence on individual politicians, and in stockpiling food, ammunition and firepower for the day when chaos came to the streets and anti-Semites sought to hang their enemies from lampposts. He had shown his father the literature, the hate sites on the internet, the books and magazines and newspapers produced by latter-day neo-Nazi organizations. In this era of social networking in which every man and woman with a computer could reach untold thousands of potential allies, those who hated Jews weren't even trying to hide anymore. They spoke freely and, worse, advocated freely for the destruction of innocent men and women.

Arguing with a man of similar ideals who lacked Eli Berwald Sr.'s experiences, Aaron might well have failed to persuade him. But his dad had watched countless friends die in Schlechterwald. He knew well the horrible end of the path that started with mindless hate. He had lived through the gradual, then meteoric rise of tensions within Germany, as Hitler scapegoated the Jews for his own ends.

"Long knives and broken glass," Aaron had told his father. "That is the future that awaits us again. We can prepare ourselves to fight, or we can let them herd us into camps to die again. Which will you choose?"

He hated using the idea against his father, to gain the man's assent, but they had to have unity of purpose in this. Reluctantly, fearing that they were perhaps likely to make matters worse, Eli Sr. had given his blessing to the new programs.

Aaron had implemented his operations immediately. There was, unknown to most Americans, a wealth of paramilitary and civilian training available online, through books and DVDs, and by contract. Selecting what he called his Lantern commandos from among their youngest, strongest and most eager new members, he first had them work through a training curriculum he had devised with materials purchased online. Recruits were taught familiarity with weapons and the basics of martial arts, safe gun handling, team tactics and the like. At that point, everything was theoretical, although in the basement shooting range at the Lantern headquarters, recruits learned to load and fire the weapons they were studying.

After this initial training, Aaron had his commandos report to various facilities in the American Midwest, several of which were in Nevada. As any civilian could, the trainees learned to fire handguns, rifles and shotguns with "tactical" skill.

For other specialized instruction Aaron contracted with several famous martial artists and knife combat personalities. There was, to his initial surprise, a thriving industry in teaching individuals the use of the blade in personal combat. From among the most famous and successful of these men and women, Aaron picked half a dozen whom he brought in to teach seminars in the newly converted Lantern gym.

It was many months before his commandos were ready—and then Aaron Berwald had no use for them. This was by design. They would simply wait until they were required to defend Lantern and its people, or take more aggressive action.

Using the celebrity bounty hunter to bring Nitzche to justice had been a compromise. Eli Sr. had wanted nothing to do with actually extracting the evil bastard from a foreign nation. Once Lantern's extensive intelligence network had identified Nitzche's properties and verified that the man was there, alive, and actually one and the same as the Klaus Nitzche of Schlechterwald, the elder Berwald had wanted to inform the authorities and leave it to them. He believed Lantern worked best wielding influence behind the scenes, poking and prodding rather than saying and doing. While that formula had served Lantern well during his father's tenure, Aaron couldn't justify continuing that lack of involvement.

Lantern would have to be ready to make changes, not merely suggest them, were it and the Jewish people to survive the dark days Aaron Berwald feared were coming. A few times, his attempts to prepare fully for that eventuality had led him into trouble. Each time, Lantern and his father had come to his aid—but the problems had only served to further darken Eli Berwald Sr.'s opinion of his son's plans. Aaron honestly didn't blame him. What father wants to worry that his son might go to jail for, say, attempting to purchase automatic weapons from a man who turned out to be a plant from the Bureau of Alcohol, Tobacco and Firearms?

But all that was different now. When the courts had proved insufficient to hold the old Nazi camp leader, and Heil Nitzche had finally made its real strength known, Aaron realized he had been right all along. He had used his commandos for relatively limited forays into the realm of direct action, earning for Lantern the reputation of vigilante group. Those minor engagements—such as raiding the corporate offices of a global bank, using the stolen data to expose that institution's commerce with the Nazi regime during World War II—were nothing compared to the full-scale invasion they were now mounting. But everything he had done, everything he had planned, seemed to have led Aaron to this very point.

It would be difficult for any man not to feel vindicated.

His father had insisted that the idea was insane. He had angrily forbade him to go to Kansas. Difficult as it was for Aaron to demonstrate the fact to his father, Eli Berwald Sr. no longer ran the Lantern. Aaron had instructed his commandos to obey his orders and told his father that, regardless of his wishes, the mission to recapture Klaus Nitzche was moving forward. The courts, the authorities, the police weren't capable of dealing with Nitzche, at least not in the interminable span of time it took to convict and imprison a man in today's "justice" system.

That left Lantern, and Aaron Berwald. They wouldn't allow Nitzche to escape. They wouldn't allow the world to forget.

Justice has a long memory, Aaron thought.

From the moment Nitzche's men had seized the courthouse, he knew that giving the Nazi to the authorities could never be anything but a disaster. Nitzche was too powerful for the legal system. They should simply have arranged to execute him for his many crimes, once he had been pulled from the safety of his Argentine lair.

This night they were going to put that right.

While the immense bunker Nitzche had managed to build in Kansas was daunting, it was nothing they couldn't deal with. Lantern had, Aaron would bet, more extensive details of Nitzche's holdings and properties than the government did. They knew where he would go to ground; they were counting on it. When the terrorist force took the courthouse, Aaron had begun placing calls, making sure there would be no official resistance to Nitzche's escape plan. Trying to stop Klaus Nitzche would only result in more lives lost. Once he was free, Lantern could go after him on their own terms.

There was the chance of a mistake; Aaron could admit that. It was possible that this warren of fortifications, created by Nitzche's people to serve as a redoubt in the United States, was still unoccupied. But it wouldn't make sense for Nitzche to spend so much time, energy and money creating a fortress he then didn't use. No, the old Nazi was here. Aaron was sure of it.

He only regretted that there had been no time to practice the raid. His people were well-trained, he believed, but still very inexperienced when it came to work of this kind. A few months to run drills in which they worked out precisely how they would take Nitzche's fortress—that would have been a blessing. Aaron realized he might as well wish for a year, and the support of helicopters and tanks, while he was at it.

So. They would fight with what they had. They would succeed. They were in the right. It was unquestionable.

Nitzche would pay for his crimes.

Behind Aaron in the tunnel was the rest of his contingent of commandos, except for the rear guard. If he had learned anything from the team tactics training, it was the importance of covering his own back. Gabriel, Malachi, Hiram and

Jeff would signal if there was any trouble, or come directly to him in the event of—

"Aaron!" Gabriel whispered from the darkness of the trench. "Aaron! We have a problem!"

Aaron cursed. This was exactly what he feared might happen: something for which they hadn't planned.

The small squad moved quietly, but they were hindered by something Aaron hadn't thought to imagine. Jeff was also nursing a knee injury of some kind, Aaron noted. The four men were prodding forward at gunpoint a prisoner, dressed in black as they were. Aaron appraised the man, not sure if he liked what he saw.

The man was big, taller than any of his people, and built very solidly. Even at gunpoint he moved with the taut menace of a panther, as if at any moment he might reach out and maul one of the men who held guns on him. His face was smeared with black greasepaint. He was laden with weaponry that Aaron's team members hadn't taken from him: an enormous knife, two large handguns—one of which Aaron recognized from the butt and extended magazine as a select-fire Beretta machine pistol—and a tricked-out American assault rifle on a sling across his chest. A heavy canvas bag was slung across his shoulder, and he wore combat webbing covered in grenades and other gear.

"Eli 'Aaron' Berwald, I presume," the man said.

"Who and what are you?" Aaron demanded.

"Cooper," he replied. "Matthew Cooper, Justice Department. You and your people are illegally holding a federal agent. You are also interfering in an officially government-sanctioned counterterror operation."

Aaron paused for a moment, digesting that. "You say you are with the Justice Department?"

"Yes."

"That's unusual. I wasn't aware our Justice Department

went around fielding black-clad commandos bearing enough armament for a one-man war."

"I could say the same of our Jewish lobbying organizations." Cooper nodded toward his captors and back to Aaron.

"You are here to argue politics?"

"No," he said. "I'm here to stop Klaus Nitzche and free the hostages he's holding."

"We are here to do the same. If you wish to assist us, we won't stop you. Don't get in our way."

"That's not how this works," Cooper said. Aaron could see a muscle connected to the man's jaw working. "I've wasted enough time with you idiots. Put down your guns and go home. Now. While you still can."

Aaron sighed. "Malachi, tie him up. We'll leave him here, out of the way, and try to come back for him when we extract."

Malachi moved forward and nudged the government agent with the barrel of his Glock pistol. "All right, you—" he said.

The moment the weapon touched Cooper, he spun, slapping the gun away, stepping in and using the lower edge of his hand to scoop up and into Malachi's throat. The man dropped, choking. The other three members of the rear guard, except for Jeff, tried to rush the government man, who became a blur of motion. He kicked one savagely in the stomach, turned, swept his arm up under Hiram's armpit and did some kind of twisting, tossing move that threw the man to the ground. He ended up against the far side of the trench wall next to Jeff and rammed an elbow into his face. The blow seemed almost an afterthought, as if Bolan were making a point.

When the former captive ripped the big knife from its sheath and was suddenly holding the blade at his throat, Aaron realized that making a point was exactly what this Matthew Cooper had in mind.

"Don't kill me," Aaron said. "We aren't your enemies."

"You're nobody's enemy, Berwald," Cooper said. "You're a child compared to the people you think you're hunting. They're going to grind you up and throw you away if you set foot in that place. You have absolutely no idea what you face here, none! You're going to *die,* Berwald, and every last one of the people with you is going to as well."

"Stand and do nothing in the face of evil, then?" Aaron said with difficulty, feeling sweat trickle down his forehead as the edge of the knife brushed his neck. He saw the rest of his half-dozen commandos start to move in, start to reach for their weapons. He very slowly held up one hand and waved them off.

"No," he said. "Don't try anything. Offer no resistance."

"I'm trying to be tolerant, Berwald," Cooper said. "You're not in my league. Your people are amateurs. Get gone, now, or the blood spilled when they're all taken out will be on your hands."

"My people are trained," Aaron said. "What they lack in experience they make up for in preparation."

"If your people were trained," Cooper retorted, "they'd have shot me the moment they set eyes on me, instead of dancing around trying to see who I was. Do you honestly think some kickboxing classes and a handful of small arms put you even with Nitzche and his thugs?"

"They're human," Aaron said. "They bleed like we all do."

Cooper withdrew the knife. "I'm continuing on," he said. "If I see you or any of your group following me, I will put you down."

He brushed past the ranks of Aaron's shaken men and disappeared into the trench beyond. Once cloaked by the shadows, it was as if he had never been there.

"Aaron?" Malachi asked, wheezing, from the ground.

Hiram, shaking but not hurt, helped him to his feet. "What do we do?"

Aaron looked after Cooper, his face growing hot.

"We do what we came here to do," he said, drawing his pistol.

7

They weren't going to listen. Bolan knew the type too well. They were stubborn and, until somebody bloodied their noses for them, they were going to insist that they knew what they were doing.

He had done all he could to discourage them. The rest was on them.

The soldier hurried through the trench until, finally, the mouth of another tunnel awaited. He would have to go underground if he were to continue. Inside, there were no lights, although there were more disconnected or unpowered task lights strung up. He used his combat light and pressed on, keeping the M-4 ready at his side on its sling.

The Executioner checked his phone every few junctions, driving deeper. The tunnel opened to a trench again before once more diving underground. The maze of passageways was very similar to one he had fought through before. That facility, too, had been a den for neo-Nazis, its most notable and dangerous feature being—

Bolan stepped on some kind of mechanical release.

Traps. The most notable feature of the maze he had walked previously had been booby traps. Had he just stepped on a land mine?

He used his light to probe the darkness at his feet. His combat boot rested on a metal trigger. He bent and very carefully scratched away some of the dirt around the sole.

It didn't look like any land mine he had seen previously. It did, however, look like an alarm trigger. To be safe, Bolan lowered his center of gravity, loading his leg muscles to spring. Then he counted off in his head.

He jumped, crashing into the far wall of the trench. Nothing exploded.

But the soldier could hear footfalls coming quickly, from before him, not behind. It had definitely been an alarm, and Nitzche's men were about to make themselves known.

So be it. He would be ready.

He was already on the floor of the trench, so he stayed there. He stretched out prone and extended the M-4 before him, sighting through the red-dot optics. The enemy were significant in number and lax in discipline. He heard them coming from some distance, muttering to one another and making what was, to Bolan, a racket as they stomped along.

He lay very still.

In the shadows, pressed against the base of the trench wall, Bolan became just another part of the semidarkness. As the oncoming force neared he could pick out detail. They carried Kalashnikov rifles and wore the same camouflage fatigues that Nitzche's terrorists at the courthouse had worn. They were moving from the direction of Nitzche's bunker.

The HN was on parade.

Bolan's finger tightened on the trigger of the carbine. Quietly, he shifted position, training his optics on the first man in line. They would close in, and then they would spot him. As they tried to acquire him with their rifles, he would send them to hell.

Except they didn't. They kept right on coming, making no change in their demeanor even when they were practically on top of the soldier. They were chattering together, trading insults, laughing. They weren't worried at all. They were safe in their fortress; what could touch them here that they couldn't repel?

Then they hurried right past him.

One man came close enough that he nearly stepped on Bolan's rifle. The Executioner let the knot of soldiers pass, and when they had walked beyond his position, he rolled onto his back and then to his knees, regaining his feet. The beams of the flashlights the men carried gave away their locations and backlit them beautifully.

The Executioner squeezed the trigger again and again, spraying out the magazine of the carbine in short, tight bursts. He ripped the enemy open from behind, pumping bullets into their spines and the backs of their heads. The M-4 cycled empty and Bolan let it fall on its sling, drawing the Desert Eagle from its Kydex holster and pumping .44 Magnum rounds into the remaining foes. He shot one in the face, another through the neck; drilled still another through the heart.

Answering fire came from the opposite end of the trench, where it opened into the tunnel he had recently traversed. Bolan pressed himself against the wall and listened as slugs dug dirt from the trench opposite his position. They came from handguns, a mixture of types and calibers. It was most likely the Lantern team. If they were targeting him, either to eliminate him or because they had mistaken his shooting for that of the neo-Nazis, they weren't doing a very effective job. He waited for the gunfire to abate and then hurried into the next tunnel.

The lights came on. Just like that, the tunnel and the trenches beyond it danced with shadows cast by the multiple hanging work lights. Bolan reloaded his M-4 as he crouch-walked ahead. There was still a long way to go.

As he suspected would happen, more clots of neo-Nazi troops began to move through the trench maze, which branched often into switchbacks and dead ends. The closer he got to the bunker, the more complex the configuration would become.

It was time Nitzche's goons got a taste of psychological warfare. Bolan reached into his war bag and produced a small radio. It was a simple AM-FM world band receiver, tuned to a local rock station. Bolan picked up his pace, found the set of cross-trenches he wanted and switched on the radio, throwing it far from him. At the end of the trench, electric guitar and driving drums began extolling the virtues or faults of someone named "Black Betty." Bolan affixed the suppressor to his Beretta 93-R and snapped the selector switch to semiautomatic.

He let the first few neo-Nazis pass his position. These men thought they were stealthy; they were crouch-walking with their Kalashnikovs held at low ready, prepared to engage as soon as they found a target. Stupidly, they were homing straight in on the music, rather than recognizing it as the decoy it clearly was.

One of them, Bolan realized, wasn't quite as stupid as the others. As if he could smell the trap, he turned his head, checking over his shoulder. The last thing he saw wasn't Bolan stepping from the shadows, extending the Beretta 93-R. No, the last thing he saw was the suppressor itself, as Bolan pushed the snout of the weapon in front of the neo-Nazi's left eye and pulled the trigger.

The clap of the suppressed Beretta would have been enough to alert the other shooters, but the warm, wet splash of their partner's brains in their ears tipped the gunmen first. Bolan gave them credit; they didn't waste time with exclamations of shock or shouted threats. They just turned to fire.

He shot each man once. At such close range, it was like a carnival game rigged in his favor.

"Oh my God!" Bolan shouted, pitching his voice slightly higher than normal. "They're dead! They're all dead!"

He moved into the next tunnel, drew his combat knife with his left hand and brought the massive blade down through the hanging cable of lights. The bulbs sparked, the rubber handle of Bolan's weapon insulating him from the surge. The tunnel was plunged into darkness.

"What happened?" someone asked.

"I can't see anything!" said another.

"Use your flashlights, morons!" a third man said.

The neo-Nazis switched on their lights—and Bolan was waiting. Flicking the Beretta's selector to 3-round burst, he fired a blast into the chest of each man foolish enough to leave his flashlight on. The hollowpoint rounds chewed through his enemies and left them dead in bloody heaps on the trench floor.

"It's so horrible!" Bolan shouted again. He ran, shooting, targeting more distant flashes of light, not caring if he scored clean hits or not. His goal was to create confusion, fear and chaos. It was part of the tradecraft of the guerrilla fighter.

Bolan was very good at what he did.

The neo-Nazis began shouting to one another. The suppressor disguised the muzzle-blast and diffused the sound of Bolan's shots. The enemy wouldn't be able to place him based on his fire.

"Who was that?"

"Morales?"

"Eaton, is that you?"

"They got Eaton! He's dead! He's dead! I never saw who did it!" Bolan shouted.

"Who said that? Eaton! Eaton!"

Bolan screamed as he ran past, doing his best bloodcurdling, wordless yell. He shot another of the men and then, sheathing his knife and pistol, withdrew three canisters from

his war bag. He pulled the pins as he sprinted for the end of
the tunnel, tossing the canisters behind him. Drawing a large
light-stick from his bag, he snapped it and tossed it after the
canisters. Then he crouched, faced the wall of the trench and
opened his mouth while covering his ears.

The flash-bang grenades rolled through the tunnel, bouncing off dead men and dirt walls. The light-stick followed,
leaving glowing green phantom trails in the air.

The flash-bangs detonated.

Bolan saw a burst of light through his eyelids, but his vision wasn't destroyed as were the senses of his enemies. In the
glow of the light-stick he targeted the men where they stood,
knelt or writhed. The man once known as Sergeant Mercy
showed these miserable soldiers of hate what true mercy was
as his bullets dug tunnels through their brains, through their
hearts or spines. The weapon was part of him. He fired it as
naturally and as effortlessly as breathing, seemingly without
conscious thought.

He was the Executioner.

Bolan had more tricks in his bag. He backtracked to the
little GP4 radio he had thrown, found it and switched it off,
pocketing it once more. It was small and light, no bigger than
the palm of his hand; he carried more than one receiver like it.
From his war bag he produced two spheres the size of metal
"meditation balls." These were made of impact-resistant clear
plastic, housing clusters of bright blue-white LEDs. They
were pocket strobes.

He heard movement at his back. It was tentative, confused;
the Lantern people had caught up. He activated the pressure
switch on one of the strobes and dropped it in his path. Farther
along, he tossed another down a side trench. Then he began
his psy-ops campaign anew, running from trench to trench,
always working his way closer to Nitzche's bunker. At each
crossway he shouted or whispered some new horror to the

men in the darkness—those foolish enough to believe they hunted Bolan, rather than the other way around.

The neo-Nazis changed their tactics at the next tunnel. He cut their lights again, but not before he saw four men at the mouth link arms. They ran at him in a phalanx, determined to crash into him in the darkness. A dumb play, though against amateurs like the Lantern operatives, it would probably work. It was just too bad for the HN thugs that Bolan had found them first.

Time to create unreasoning terror in the opposition. They had to believe the trenches were the dominion of some unspeakable wraith, some unstoppable, unseen killing machine. Bolan took no pleasure in it, but for one man to defeat many, it was necessary. He stowed the Beretta.

Bolan dropped to one knee, braced the M-4 and chopped the legs out from under the phalanx. He rolled to the side to avoid the panic fire that followed. The soldier was no longer where his muzzle-blast had been. Bullets punched useless holes in the dirt.

In the darkness, as the strobe lights flashed, the black-clad soldier moved like a stop-motion monster crawling from a horror movie. There were screams from the wounded neo-Nazis and those nearby witnessing the attack as Bolan fell upon them.

The Executioner waded into them with a blade. They weren't unarmed; they had pistols and one had a rifle slung over his shoulder. One of the unlucky four even tried to draw his own blade in response to the threat, perhaps believing that stabbing randomly in the strobing fever-dream of the tunnel, he could succeed where aimed fire had so far failed. Bolan's blade went in and out, in and out, across and down. Blood sprayed. The screams of the dying were joined by screams of fear from the other men in the tunnels and trenches.

"He's insane!" Bolan shouted through the darkness. "Run! Run! Nothing can stop him!"

"Go, go, go!" someone screamed from among the neo-Nazis forces.

"Call for backup! Call for backup!"

The rest of the screams weren't screams at all, but blind gunfire as the HN cowards emptied their weapons into the darkness. Bolan stayed low, crawling on his belly, his knife in his fist as he wormed his way along. The strobes, which had limited power sources, had stopped now. The only illumination was from the flashlight beams of the shooters. A second cluster of lights was moving up the trench from far behind. That would be the Lantern people, who had bunched up so badly they were sitting ducks should anyone decide to trigger a blast into their midst.

The soldier crawled forward. A new group of neo-Nazis was filing down the trench, trying to cover each other's flanks with their guns. Bolan moved straight up the middle, his blacksuit camouflaging him effectively. The men were night-blind, relying on the flashlights they carried. They were sweeping the beams ahead at chest level, not watching the ground.

That was their mistake. Bolan slashed out with his big, up-swept blade, cutting their hamstrings, dropping them in place like broken marionettes. As they fell, shocked, reeling from the pain and momentarily confused as to what had happened, they had no time to react. Bolan brought the knife up and down, stabbing the men in turn, driving his blade through the hollow of a throat, through an eye socket, through an abdomen. He worked like a well-oiled machine, silent and deadly, letting his knife speak for him.

Several neo-Nazis were concentrated at the end of the tunnel. Bolan realized the ambient light was increasing again. He was rising as he worked his way through the trench network.

That meant he was getting closer to his goal. He used a side passage near him for cover as he pitched a high-explosive grenade at the cluster of enemy gunners.

The blast that followed ripped through the ranks of neo-Nazis. They broke and ran, finally. The ones who were still mobile fled in stark terror, running for their lives along the trench.

Bolan peered cautiously from his vantage. A large steel door blocked the passage leading forward. He checked his phone. He was at the very perimeter of Nitzche's bunker now, a stone's throw from the structure itself. His running, crawling, creeping gun battle had brought him to the old Nazi's doorstep.

Sudden gunfire took him by surprise, because it was pointed in the wrong direction. His sense of hearing, which was much better than it had any right to be, considering his exposure to high decibels during combat, told him that farther along the trench-and-tunnel network, a new firefight was ongoing…and it didn't involve him.

Lantern. They had finally found the action they were so eager to involve themselves in.

Bolan glanced at the steel door and then back through the trenches. He had told the Lantern operatives they would face death and destruction. He had made it clear they were out of their league. He had no obligation to save them.

But he couldn't leave them. They weren't bad people; they were merely misguided and in over their heads. They wanted to bring men like Nitzche to justice regardless of the legal system's ability to do so…and what was Bolan if not an avatar of the very same ideal?

"Heaven save us from amateurs," he muttered. Shouldering his M-4, he stalked down the trench, ready to acquire targets.

He was halfway there when the gunfire stopped. In the dim light of the trench he saw figures locked in personal combat, stabbing and punching and striking. The fight had devolved from weapons to hand-to-hand. He couldn't tell, in this light, a camouflage uniform from a black one.

He let his rifle fall and drew his knife once more. Spinning it in his palm, he reversed it, locking his fingers around the handle in a clenched fist. In his other hand, he grasped his combat light, blinking the bright light on and off with the thumb cap switch, moving each time he illuminated his position. He worked methodically, pulling each knot of fighting men apart and driving his blade into the throat or chest of the neo-Nazi. He did this twice before a Lantern operative came at him blindly—the one named Malachi. Bolan threw a piston front-kick into the young man's abdomen that left him retching on the floor of the trench.

When he got to Berwald, he paused. The leader had dispatched his opponent with a slash of his own blade. He and Bolan stood regarding each other, grasping their knives. Aaron held a long, thin, double-edged dagger, a Fairbairn-Sykes combat knife.

"Your move," Bolan said.

Berwald collapsed against the trench wall. He was breathing heavily. The other Lanterns gathered around. Aaron looked wild-eyed in the dim light. The soldier realized then what was wrong. Of the Lantern contingent, only three had survived: Berwald, Malachi and the operative named Hershel. The trench was littered with bodies, as was the tunnel to which it connected.

Bolan reached out and offered the leader a hand up.

"Get away from me!" Berwald screamed in horror. "I saw! I saw what you did!"

Bolan stared. Had Berwald cracked? He didn't have time for this. He turned to Malachi and Hershel, who looked shell-shocked. He reached out and grabbed Malachi by the collar, prepared to have to fight the man. Malachi simply looked at him, dumbfounded.

"Take care of him," Bolan ordered. "Do you hear me? Malachi! See to your leader. Aaron needs you."

"Y-yeah." Malachi nodded slowly. "Yes. Yes, I will. Please…please don't hurt me."

Bolan released the man. "Stay here. Unless you want to see what's left of your friends die." The soldier turned to leave.

"Cooper," Malachi called after him. "What makes you better than them? How can a man… How can a man kill like that and not become a monster? Not *be* a creature of hate?"

"Because if they put their guns down," Bolan said, "I'd take them in. If I put my guns down, they'll kill me. It's Israel and its radical enemies all over again, kid. If the enemies of Israel laid down their arms tomorrow, the region would coexist in peace."

"But if Israel surrendered her own military…" Malachi said softly.

"The streets would run red with blood in days."

"I…I think I understand," Malachi murmured.

"You're starting to, kid," Bolan said. "You're starting to."

8

The steel door was as he had left it. Bolan checked the perimeter for obvious traps or sensors and, finding nothing, decided the direct approach was best.

The compact, remote-detonated charges were yet another toy designed by the specialists at Stony Man Farm, in this case by Cowboy Kissinger and Gadgets Schwarz in tandem. Kissinger had put together the payload, while the compact detonator was a piece of electronic wizardry designed by Schwarz. The charges had both a contact adhesive and, when charged, a powerful electromagnet. Bolan clicked the chargers and let two of the bombs adhere to the metal skin of the barrier. Then he retreated to the cover of the closest trench.

There was no sign of Berwald or his two surviving operatives.

Bolan pushed the switch on the remote detonator.

The explosion made his ears ring. A tornado of superheated air ripped past as the doors were blown clear, setting off some kind of alarm that reminded Bolan of mechanical school bells.

Through the smoke and debris marched the Executioner.

He was standing in a subbasement with a dirt floor. The walls were concrete; there were bare bulbs hanging from fixtures in the ceiling. Crude targets had been spray-painted on

the walls. It was a makeshift shooting range. Bolan stepped
closer to one of the targets and inhaled.

Blood.

He'd thought as much. The dark red stains blotching the
concrete walls could be little else. His face dark with anger,
Bolan kicked spent shells with his combat boots. Unlike
those that now littered the maze of trenches beyond the bunker, these were old, many of them tarnished. There was no
telling how many people Nitzche and his private army had
killed here. Some of them might have been hostages from
the courthouse. Bolan didn't want to think just how many of
those Nitzche had kidnapped might have suffered under the
neo-Nazi's cruelty.

The soldier found a concrete stairwell leading upward.
There was no guard at the door. He emerged into a large room
at ground level and was amazed by what he saw: pool tables
and pinball machines; a full bar along one wall. A small stage,
complete with stripper poles, dominated the opposite wall.
Track lighting and even a karaoke machine had been set up
here. It was a recreation room.

Opposite the stairs to the subbasement was a set of heavy
wooden double doors. Bolan started for these.

The doors opened.

"Well, well, well," Klaus Nitzche said. "It seems I owe you
that five dollars after all, Indio. One of the fools survived."

The old Nazi was dressed like a retired socialite, in silk
pajamas, slippers and a smoking jacket. He held a carved
ivory pipe in one hand.

He held an ornately engraved Luger pistol in the other.

Stony Man Farm's intelligence files had included a
workup—extracted with great difficulty, considering
Nitzche's discretion—of the old Nazi's known associates.
Bolan recognized the Uruguayan, who had traveled with
Nitzche for some years. Known in the files only as Indio,

the man was enormous and, if half the crimes attributed to him were true, an almost pathological killer, rumored to have murdered at least a dozen people with his bare hands and with knives.

Nitzche, guarded by Indio, was flanked by several of his camouflage-clad neo-Nazi thugs. The HN members fanned out to either side. There were more of them filing in behind Nitzche. They had been waiting, which explained the lack of guards in the lower level.

"He doesn't have the look of one of Berwald's scuttling rats," Nitzche said, appraising Bolan. "He seems rather more…professional. Don't you think?"

Indio's expression hardened. His eyes locked on Bolan's. "My leader," he said quietly, "give me leave to kill this man. Now. While it can be done."

"Eh?" Nitzche looked up at Indio. "Why, Indio, I've never seen that look on your face before. Do I detect a note of…?" Nitzche thought better of speaking the word, perhaps to prevent Indio from losing face in front of the other HN personnel. But Bolan and the old Nazi both knew the look on Indio's face.

It was fear.

"Tell the men to shoot," Indio urged. "Tell them to shoot now, my leader. Or let me do it. But don't let that one leave this room."

"What is the matter with you, Indio?" Nitzche appeared perplexed. "He can do nothing. We hold all the cards. Isn't this what we've been waiting for? The night's entertainment, come to our doorstep at last?"

Just then, another neo-Nazi rushed into the room, carrying a two-way radio and looking very pale. He came up behind Indio and spoke very quietly to the HN lieutenant. Indio nodded, never taking his eyes from Bolan.

"Sir," said Indio to Nitzche. "Report from the trench network, sir. Our men report that we have lost nine of every ten men, sir."

Nitzche turned red. He stared at Indio as if the man had just accused him of being Jewish. "Are you *insane?* Nine of ten would be—"

"More than you can afford to lose," Bolan said. "And they're all dead because of me."

"Who are you?" Nitzche demanded.

"Matthew Cooper," Bolan said. "Justice Department. Surrender now to my custody and nobody else has to die."

Nitzche froze. His men stared at him. Finally, the old Nazi began to tremble. When he finally made a noise, it came out as a cackle.

The old man was literally shaking with laughter.

That was when Berwald, Malachi and Hershel burst in, pistols in their hands.

"Nobody move!" Berwald screamed. "We hereby place you under citizen's arrest!"

Bolan started to move, but Indio had anticipated him, crossing the space and clamping one large hand around Hershel's throat. He kicked Malachi and Berwald aside contemptuously, holding Hershel out before him like a shield.

"Draw a weapon, government man," Indio roared, "and I will snap his neck."

"Don't hurt him," Aaron Berwald said. He put his weapon on the floor. Malachi did the same.

The HN troops had all raised their automatic weapons. Bolan was covered by more guns than even he could outfight. He knew it and Indio knew it, too.

"Good boy," the Uruguayan said.

There was an earsplitting crack.

Hershel's corpse fell to the floor.

"No!" Berwald screamed, rushing forward.

Nitzche, still cackling, shot him three times. Berwald

crumpled. When Indio drew a short, concealed bowie knife from his pocket and slashed Malachi across the throat, the last of the Lantern operatives barely reacted. He simply gurgled and died, folding where he stood.

Indio grinned. Some of his confidence was returning. He had just murdered two men this "Cooper" considered allies, and there had been no reprisal. He was emboldened. Bolan saw that in his eyes, in the way he carried himself.

"I would have given his father more credit," Nitzche said. "Sending children to do the job of soldiers, to fight other soldiers. Of course we massacred them."

"Just like I massacred your men," Bolan said. He clenched his fists, feeling righteous wrath building inside him.

"No matter," Nitzche said. "I will see to it that Mr. Berwald Sr. pays for the extreme difficulty he has caused me. Killing his son is just the start."

"You're scum, Nitzche," Bolan said. "They might have been amateurs, but they were better men than you or any of your thugs."

"Fool!" Nitzche said. "The United States government wishes to show me how strong it is, and so it sends one man! One man with delusions of his own strength!"

"I'm stronger than you," Bolan said. "And your men know it."

Nitzche's face darkened. "No man challenges my strength. It is the constant of my life."

"Your life," Bolan told him, "is coming to an end. And they all know it. How much longer do you have, Klaus? You could have easily died in prison."

"I will show you strength!" Nitzche roared. "Indio! Bring me that idiot Orwin." He gestured to his men. "Lay down your guns, Cooper. You may keep your other weapons. We are going to have the evening's promised entertainment, and my men are going to avenge themselves on you the way men of *strength* do."

Bolan stepped to one of the pool tables. He unclipped the M-4 from its single point sling and placed it on the table. His Beretta and his Desert Eagle followed. When he turned, Indio had come back, pushing a thin, dark-haired man in a sweat-stained three-piece suit.

"Please, please, please don't kill me," Kevin Orwin begged. Bolan recognized him from the profile the Farm had sent to him before the courthouse operation. He was Nitzche's attorney.

"This," Nitzche said, "is a man of weakness. A sniveling coward, interested only in saving his own hide. Watch." He turned to Orwin, who had of course heard every word just spoken. "Tell me, Kevin, if I gave you this pistol and asked you to shoot every one of your fellow hostages, would you do it? Such a demonstration of loyalty would ensure your freedom."

"Y-yes sir, yes sir," Orwin said from his knees. "Anything, Mr. Nitzche. Anything you say."

"You see, Cooper?" Nitzche said with a sneer. "These are the men working for your government, for your vaunted justice system. Are these the creatures you believe you are defending? Are they the worms you serve? They are weak, and so are you." He gestured with the Luger, offering it grip-first to Orwin, who looked up, hesitating.

"He's nothing," Bolan said. "Let him go. He's not worth a bullet."

"Oh, I beg to differ," Nitzche replied. His crocodile smile turned to a grimace of shame. "I languished in a freezing cell for *months* while this idiot prattled on, pretending to be defending me. He was simply biding his time, collecting his pay. He is a tool of the state. He isn't expected to bring about justice. He is there so your government may go through the motions, pay lip service to its ideals, while prosecuting great men such as myself."

"No, sir, please, I'll do anything you ask," Orwin whined.

"Oh, do shut up," Nitzche said. He shot Orwin once in the forehead, spraying the man's brains over the tiled floor of the recreation room. Orwin stared up at the ceiling, his expression one of surprise and terror.

"You didn't have to do that," Bolan said darkly.

"He died as he lived," Nitzche replied. "A worthless tub of guts."

"And that's how you show your strength?" Bolan asked. "By shooting unarmed men?"

"No," Nitzche said. "This is how—by walking away while my men beat you to death. Come, Indio. The men have earned their amusement, especially in light of their…fallen brothers. We have much planning to discuss."

"Sir, I was hoping…"

"Hmm? Oh, yes. Of course. The court reporter. Yes, our business can wait, Indio." He patted the giant on one thickly veined forearm. "You go and play, loyal Indio. You've earned it."

"Are you certain you won't reconsider?" Indio looked back at Bolan. "I would prefer he die immediately."

"You worry too much, Indio," Nitzche said. "I won't deprive the men. It's this or the shooting range and, frankly, I think this is the more fitting redress."

"Yes, my leader," Indio rumbled. He followed Nitzche from the room, but not before shooting one last death stare at Bolan.

The double doors locked behind them.

The neo-Nazis attacked.

They lowered their pistols and submachine guns, slinging them. From their belts and pockets they drew knives.

Bolan slid his combat dagger from its sheath.

"Well," he said, "come on, then, if you're coming."

They charged.

The soldier bobbed and weaved, ducked and slipped. Blades came at him from every angle. He slapped at fore-arms and elbows, stabbing with short, sharp, digging motions, using his enemies' body mechanics against them. For every move, there was a counter. For every arc of the human arm, there was a means of cutting, of stabbing, to intercept. Bolan was the most experienced knife fighter any of these men would ever face; he had drawn blades in life-and-death battle countless times during his war.

A dozen men against Mack Bolan was hardly fair at all... to them.

He drew his blade against the arm of one attacker, using a scissors motion that practically deboned the enemy's limb. He used the butt of the knife to strike another man's arm up and over, then drew the reversed blade across the man's throat.

He cut a weapon from a neo-Nazi's hand by slicing the tendons on the back.

Blood sprayed; men screamed. Bolan fought them all, his economy of movement bewildering to behold. It was as if his movements were choreographed as he slid among them like oiled death and rended limbs, speared throats, opened guts. He picked one man up and threw him onto the bar, dragging him across the glassware there, to land in a heap at the other end. The soldier stabbed a third through the eye socket and pinned him to the pool table—the pool table bearing Mack Bolan's weapons.

Too late, the few surviving neo-Nazis realized their mistake. Bolan snatched up his pistols and fired, two-handed, in two directions at once, splitting skulls and punching open chests.

When the Executioner ran out of human targets, he whirled, targeted the karaoke machine and pumped the last of his .44 Magnum bullets into it, on principle alone.

Then there was silence.

Bolan stood, breathing heavily, his clothes covered in the blood of his enemies, his pistol barrels burning. He was surrounded by the dead.

"It isn't might that makes right," he said to no one. "Strength flows from justice."

"And justice," said a soft voice, "has a long memory."

Bolan followed the sound and found Aaron Berwald on the floor. He was critically wounded. Blood flowed from his mouth. Even if he were lying in an emergency room, there would be no way to save him. He was dying.

"Cooper," he said.

"I'm here, kid," Bolan told him. He helped Berwald into a half-sitting position against the wall.

"I screwed up," Aaron Berwald said. "They're...they're all dead, Cooper."

"That's war," Bolan stated. "People die. Good people. More than you'll ever believe you can lose and still go on."

"I'm...sorry," Berwald said. "I shouldn't have...tried... to make justice."

Bolan closed his eyes. When he opened them again, he looked straight at the dying Aaron Berwald and made a decision.

"I want to tell you something before you go, Aaron," he said. "You weren't ready. You weren't prepared. But the urge for justice, to want to do what's right, is never wrong. Don't die believing that."

"But I lost...everyone...."

"And I've lost people, too," Bolan said.

"How do you...live with it?" Berwald was very close to the end now.

"They died for what was right, too. In their own way, every one of them fought with me. Even the ones who never picked up a gun."

"My...ring..." Berwald gasped. He was wearing a gold ring of ornate design. It looked very old.

"Yes?" Bolan asked.

"My...father...gave it to me...." Berwald said. "When I...took over...Lantern. Please give it back to him. And tell him..."

Bolan waited. Aaron Berwald stared at nothing. He was dead.

"Yeah, kid," Bolan said. "I'll tell him."

9

When Bolan found the soundproof room where the hostages were being kept, he understood why none of Nitzche's men had reacted to the massacre in the recreation room. That was so typical of these supremacist types, Bolan thought. Arrogance and overconfidence were frequently their undoing.

He had stuck his knife through the necks of a pair of lazy sentries to get here, but for the most part, Nitzche and his thugs believed themselves to be safe. It made a certain sense. The invasion by enemy forces they had anticipated had come, and the intruders had been defeated. Lantern's best vigilante force had been fielded and destroyed. The government, which the members of HN so feared and hated, was represented by Bolan, and he, too, had been neutralized. There were probably hidden cameras in the recreation room. Possibly Nitzche had seen to the murder of other victims in that room, and Bolan wouldn't be surprised if there was a room full of recordings of each of those deaths. The arrangement Nitzche had built for captives only strengthened that suspicion.

The old Nazi had taken the time to build or, more accurately, have built, an elaborate two-way mirror setup, not unlike a police interrogation room. Actually, the more Bolan looked at it, the more it resembled the viewing theaters used for state executions. On one side of the one-way glass, an observation room with couches and chairs had been set up.

On the other, a large cinder-block holding cell contained the hostages taken from the courthouse.

Bolan recognized the prosecutor. Lars Kinsey was an old friend of Hal Brognola's and he had sent a lot of people to prison.

Bolan didn't see the court reporter. Her name, according to the files, was Jennifer Galloway. Counting the entrance he had used to access this viewing room, there were three exits total. One was the connecting door to the cell. The other was, according to the Farm's thermal imaging, a small room large enough for storage or...a bedroom.

Trust Nitzche to have a purpose-built holding cell complete with voyeur glass and attached rape room. Bolan contained his disgust. He went to that door and listened.

He could hear the sounds of a struggle, and a woman's protests. She sounded as if she was screaming through a pillow.

Very carefully, he tried the door. The knob didn't move under his hand. He removed his lock picks from a pouch on his blacksuit. Slowly, quietly, he began to jimmy the lock open.

The doorknob finally gave under pressure, turning to the right.

Bolan stepped inside the room. The giant, Indio, was on the bed, holding Jennifer Galloway down. He was indeed smothering her with a pillow, and had been about to pull off her skirt. The angle was bad and, given the height of the bed, it was easy enough for Indio to drag the court reporter in front of him.

The giant looked up into the barrel of Bolan's suppressed 93-R. He shifted Galloway so that she completely shielded him.

"I will dump all twenty rounds into you if I have to," Bolan warned.

"Not much room in here to fight," Indio said, grunting.

"I'm not going to fight you, either," Bolan said. "You're too big and too strong. I can't afford to play with you. I'll just have to kill you."

"Not an easy shot," Indio pointed out.

"I've made worse," Bolan replied.

They stared each other down for a long moment before Indio finally shrugged. He gave Galloway a push, dumping her on the floor in front of Bolan. The soldier helped her up. She wasn't hurt.

"Take her," Indio said. "I can get another."

"Just like that?" Bolan asked.

"You would kill me." Indio shrugged. He was completely certain. The killer in Indio recognized the counter-predator in Bolan. The big man was taking no chances. As he slowly reached under the mattress, Bolan shot him in the forehead.

The soldier clapped his hand over Galloway's mouth before she could scream. She looked at him, wide-eyed, terrified. Bolan managed to get her to calm down before he released her.

"Quietly," he said. "The others aren't far away."

"You murdered him in cold blood!" she whimpered.

"He was reaching for a weapon under the mattress. And he was going to rape you," Bolan said. "Would you rather I had left you to him?"

"No, but—" Galloway shook her head "—didn't you have a deal? You let him live and he lets me go?"

"All bets were off when he made his move. Besides, I couldn't leave him alive and mobile to come at us from behind. Nitzche still has a lot of men up and walking, and he's in the next room. Come on."

They moved back to the observation room. Bolan walked up to the glass, holstering his Beretta and selecting the .44 Magnum Desert Eagle. He would need firepower to punch through the thick glass and still take out targets beyond.

Nitzche was there now, waving his Luger, flanked by his guards and clearly enjoying himself. His words, and the voices of the hostages, were transmitted to the observation room by speakers, obviously connected to a pickup in the holding room.

"And so I have come to inform you that the amusements you afford my men are drawing to a close," Nitzche was saying. "You are here, and suffering, because you are instruments of the corrupt legal system that sought to punish me. I, in my strength, have turned the tables, and now I punish you."

"You sure talk a lot, little man," Lars Kinsey said. He was rubbing his arm and shoulder as if they pained him, but managed to stand at his full height with quiet dignity as Nitzche stared him down.

"Little man?" the old Nazi exclaimed. "Little man? I am Klaus Reinhardt Nitzche! I command an army! I was the terror of Schlechterwald!"

"I've dumped bigger things than you after a heavy breakfast," Kinsey said, sneering. He ran three fingers through his salt-and-pepper beard.

"You insolent whelp!" Nitzche said. He pointed the Luger. "I came here to kill one of you. Now I know which one it shall be!"

"Tell me something I don't know, Colonel Obvious," Kinsey said. He winced as if he had pulled a muscle. "'Insolent whelp?' Who talks like that? You're like some central casting villain from a black-and-white movie."

"Movies? You want *movies?* I have many in my collection. In each of them, one or more of my enemies is dying!"

"Do you always spend this much time giving speeches?" Kinsey demanded. "Or is this something that gets worse with age? Because you are a wrinkly old bastard, at that."

Nitzche stopped talking. Bolan saw his finger tighten on the trigger of the Luger.

"Hurry up and shoot me, already," Kinsey said. "I'm getting damned tired of waiting."

Bolan fired.

The .44 Magnum bullet tore through the one-way glass and would have hit Nitzche. At the moment Bolan chose to fire, however, the Nazi was raising his Luger to pistol-whip the belligerent prosecutor. The round meant to take the old man's hand off at the wrist instead punched through one of his guards, splitting his neck and nearly decapitating him.

Nitzche ran for the door while his men returned fire.

Bolan emptied the .44 Magnum pistol, aiming for the guards, but really more interested in punching his way through the glass barrier. Reloading the weapon, he lowered his shoulder and bulled his way through, sending pebbles of glass in every direction. Bolan paused just long enough to shoot first one, then a second neo-Nazi guard, cracking open their sternums with the Desert Eagle's powerful rounds.

"Help us! Help us!" one of the hostages cried. She was an older woman. He remembered her face from his briefing: Joyce Caldwell, an assistant to the late Kevin Orwin. She was kneeling next to the supine form of Lars Kinsey.

"What's happening here?" Bolan asked. He went to one knee next to Kinsey and checked for a pulse. There was none. Galloway joined him and, without being prompted, started CPR.

"It's his heart," Caldwell said. Tears began to stream down her cheeks. "He...he knew they were coming to kill one of us. Nitzche, that sick bastard, gets off on it. He likes to do it himself. Lars knew they were coming to take one of us. He angered Nitzche on purpose, tried to draw the old man's attention. He sacrificed himself for the rest of us."

"How long had he been having chest pains?" Bolan asked.

"All morning." Caldwell shook her head. "I think he knew.

He never said a word about it. He just stood between the bad guys and us."

Galloway stopped giving CPR. She looked to Bolan and shook her head. She was crying silently.

The soldier nodded soberly. "Thank you for trying."

"I'm sorry I couldn't do more," she said.

"Stay here," Bolan told the hostages. He went to the dead neo-Nazis and collected their weapons, producing two pistols and a micro-Uzi. "Who here can use a gun?"

Three men and Caldwell raised their hands. Bolan handed out the weapons, skipping the most nervous-looking of the male hostages.

"What do you want us to do?" Caldwell asked.

"I've got work ahead," Bolan said. "Stay here. Help will come. Nitzche's forces are depleted and he's on the run now. You should be relatively safe until I can have backup brought in to sweep this place. Watch the doors and, if you have to, choose a room with only one door and shoot whoever sticks their head in…unless it's the cavalry, of course."

"Mister?" Galloway called after him.

He looked at her over his shoulder.

"Thank you," she said. "I didn't say thank you."

Bolan nodded and hurried on.

The shotgun blast nearly took his head off when he hit the next corridor.

Nitzche wasn't stupid. He had left several men behind in an attempt to kill Bolan and cover his own retreat. He had demonstrated more than once that he was an able tactician. The exit route Nitzche had taken led to the rear of the bunker, which, above ground level, resembled a stone house. Bolan had memorized the basic layout well enough to know that a dormitory of sorts, followed by a cafeteria and a kitchen, lay between him and what he assumed was Nitzche's goal: an extensive carport sheltering the motor pool. From there, a dirt road led across the property, ultimately leading to Highway 400.

Once on that road, there was a good chance Nitzche could escape. Bolan didn't intend to let it happen a second time.

He had rescued the hostages and broken the back of Nitzche's organization, at least insofar as the fortress here in Kansas went. While the old Nazi still had ample soldiers to fight by his side, the power of Heil Nitzche was considerably attenuated.

Bolan could, he knew, trust to time and old age to do in Klaus Nitzche. With so many men and resources lost, and exposed to the authorities as he now was, Nitzche would probably attempt to emigrate back to Argentina, there to live out what remained of his days. That was the most logical scenario. Old age might kill Klaus Nitzche sooner rather than later.

But Bolan couldn't just forget the man. Not now, not ever. Not knowing that good people, innocent people, people doing their jobs in and out of the United States legal system, had died at his sick whims. Even actively hunted for the rest of his days, Nitzche would know something like peace if he was permitted to dig in and hide again. The Executioner couldn't permit that, couldn't live with the thought of it.

Pressed against the wall, Bolan waited as the shotgunner triggered another round into the wall. There was a distinct click-clack between shots, then another blast. A pump gun. While the gunman was trying to jack a new shell into the chamber of his weapon, Bolan broke from cover, punching the man through the neck with a .44 Magnum hollowpoint round.

The pump gun hit the floor. Bolan, about to enter the dormitory used by Nitzche's men, paused when the fallen weapon caught his eye. Kneeling, he lifted it and eyed it curiously. The strange-looking gun had a flashlight mount and a squared handle, like that of a chain saw. The muzzle of the shotgun was affixed with a crenellated breaching ring. The weapon resembled nothing so much as the bastard offspring of a pump gun and a chain saw.

"Now I've seen everything," Bolan muttered.

He rose to his feet and listened at the closed door to the dormitory, a hollow-core model, cheap and easily broken. He could hear the opposition muttering to one another. They were lying in wait for him, doubtless because Nitzche had instructed them to do so.

Bolan kicked the door in but didn't dive through. His action prompted a firestorm, as the neo-Nazis inside emptied their weapons. Bullets chewed the door apart, spraying splinters through the corridor. The soldier waited, counting. Sustained fire could be maintained for only so long before magazines cycled dry, and when they did...

The Executioner dived, rolling through the opening, ignored the ragged edges of the door still clinging to the hinges, and came up firing. The M-4 snarled like a buzzsaw as he fired bursts of 5.56 mm death from the barrel.

As he stalked through the dormitory, bullets ripped up through the mattresses of two of the bunk beds. The terrorists were under the beds, concealing themselves, trying to catch him in a cross fire. He knelt and wrenched the first bed up and over, pinning the man beyond. Then he turned and stitched the second mattress, emptying the M-4's magazine. A rapidly spreading pool of blood stained the floor.

Bolan switched out magazines. He made a circuit of the room, shooting whatever moved. Finally, when he'd completed his circle, he stood over the man pinned by the bed. His leg had been caught at an odd angle. Bloody bone jutted through the skin.

Bolan stepped on the handgun the man was reaching for. The neo-Nazi looked up at him and snarled.

Bolan delivered a mercy round, shooting him through the head.

He hit the kitchen cafeteria at a run. It was a big, wide-open space, with little opportunity for cover. Where cover couldn't be had, mobility would have to do. He switched to a crouch-walk in midstride, moving smoothly heel to toe, the M-4 carbine shouldered and ready.

They thought they were going to surprise him. The neo-Nazis had arrayed themselves behind the long plank tables, bracing their weapons on the tabletops. As he cruised through the room, they tried to take Bolan out, but failed to lead him sufficiently.

He was mobile. They were stationary. It was no contest.

The Executioner shot them, sweeping his carbine left and right, ignoring their return fire. If a bullet was to find him, so be it; he was long overdue. He would accept his fate.

When the soldier reached the kitchen, his carbine was empty again. He reached for a spare magazine from his web gear.

The cleaver sang as it plunged past him, narrowly missing him, striking sparks from the stainless-steel frame of the industrial-size sink behind him. The neo-Nazi let out a battle cry and tried once more to plant the heavy, square blade in his adversary's head. He collided with the soldier and pressed him back against the sink. Bolan had just enough time to get a hand up and block the arm. The edge of the cleaver hung suspended above his face.

"You're going to die today," the neo-Nazi gritted. His shaved head and face bore the same length of stubble. He used both hands to try to drive the blade into Bolan's skull.

"Hand free," the soldier said.

"Huh?" The neo-Nazi looked confused.

"I *said*—" Bolan nodded to his right hand "—I've got a hand free." He yanked his combat dagger from its sheath and plunged it into the terrorist's stomach, jerking the blade over, up and in. Blood, hot and wet, gushed over his hand and arm. The neo-Nazi collapsed, bleeding out.

10

The motor pool was empty when he got there. Bolan searched the bays. One Jeep remained in the multiunit carport, but its tires had been slashed, most likely by Nitzche to cover his escape. Bolan looked left, then right, assessing his options.

A tarp covered an object next to the far wall. He went to it and pulled it off. The Nazi, in his haste to flee, had forgotten this, or perhaps thought it unimportant. It was a Kawasaki KLX and the keys were in the ignition.

The vehicle roared to life under him when Bolan gave it some gas.

He exited the motor pool and pushed the bike as fast as he dared for the terrain. Nitzche and his men had a head start, but it wasn't insurmountable. Taking the compact field glasses from a pouch on his web gear, the soldier scanned the road ahead and spotted the dust cloud raised by the fleeing vehicles. The preceding weeks had been very dry.

Nitzche and his men were traveling in heavy four-door Jeeps. Bolan's Kawasaki was considerably faster. He leaned forward, riding out the ruts, pouring on the speed. When they saw him, they started shooting from the windows of their vehicles.

"Jack, I need you!" Bolan said. "Striker to G-Force, requesting air support this position, south of the bunker!"

"I read you, Sarge," Grimaldi said. "I'm already on my way to… Sarge! I'm getting a tone that says I'm locked!"

Bolan looked back to see the plume of the rocket rising from the bunker. There were still men in there somewhere, and they had what Bolan guessed were Stinger antiaircraft missiles.

The Cobra heeled about and deployed countermeasures, going low to avoid the rocket. Bolan couldn't see what happened next; the bunker itself was between him and his line of sight to Grimaldi. He heard and saw the explosion, however.

"Jack! Talk to me!"

"Still here, Sarge," Grimaldi reported through Bolan's transceiver. "But it looks like the intelligence was dead-on. They've got Stingers and a good field of fire. I can't get close enough to hose them clean without risking them taking a shot at me."

"Don't try, Jack," Bolan said. "I've got this."

"I can try to make a run at them," Grimaldi suggested. "All I need is long enough to line them up, and then I can raise the roof on that joint."

"If you can get a shot, go ahead and take it," Bolan said. "But don't risk yourself. We need you."

"And my chopper," Grimaldi cracked.

"And your chopper," Bolan agreed.

Bullets struck pieces of lime-green plastic from the Kawasaki, narrowly missing Bolan. He weaved back and forth along the roadway, making himself harder to target. As he neared the rear Jeep, he saw the neo-Nazis within, aiming their folding-stock Kalashnikov rifles.

Nitzche had to have lucked into a fire sale on the things, Bolan thought, which wasn't surprising. There were parts of the world where fully automatic AK rifles could be purchased for less than 20 USD each. The weapons had been plentiful on the open market even before the power vacuum created by the collapsing Soviet Union flooded world arms markets with surplus Russian hardware.

The road began to grow more difficult. Bolan started to lose ground as the Kawasaki's ability to cope with the terrain paled in comparison to the four-wheel-drive Jeeps. Automatic gunfire poured from the open windows of the neo-Nazis' vehicles, making it that much harder for the soldier. He had to try to maintain his speed while dodging the worst of the ruts and holes, all while trying not to be shot in the process.

There was no point waiting any longer. He snapped open the breech of the grenade launcher attached to his carbine, aimed from the hip and fired.

The shot was inaccurate, with both vehicles moving, but it had the desired effect. The grenade struck the rear driver's-side tire of the last Jeep and detonated, blowing it apart, sending the vehicle flipping up and over. It crashed in the middle of the roadway, a pyre for the men trapped inside. Bolan barely had time to dodge to one side and skirt the burning wreckage.

Seeing their fellows die prompted the men in the next Jeep to hose down the road. A curtain of bullets cut Bolan off; he brought the bike up short, skidding to a stop, almost laying it down. The engine stalled.

The Jeep stopped, backed to the side and then completed its turn, roaring full speed at Bolan.

The enraged neo-Nazis were going to run him down.

He stood as if frozen. Bullets struck nearby, but they were less a danger now than the bouncing, speeding Jeep itself. Bolan waited with his arms outstretched and his knees slightly bent, balancing on the balls of his feet inside his combat boots.

If he ran in any direction, he would find no cover. He would not be able to get the Kawasaki restarted and up to speed in time. He couldn't tip the driver to his maneuver until the last moment.

"Well," Bolan said, "come on if you're coming."

The grille of the Jeep bore down on him. At the last instant, he threw himself to the side. The vehicle flew past, sideswiping the burning wreckage behind Bolan. The Executioner popped back up and, targeting the rear window of the Jeep with his M-4 carbine, held back the trigger with the weapon on full-automatic.

The glass of the Jeep's rear window splintered, becoming a spiderweb red with blood. Bolan kept shooting, turning the interior of the vehicle into a kill zone of pebbled glass and flying lead. He looked behind him, forward up the road. The Jeeps protecting and conveying Nitzche were getting farther away by the moment.

The one he had just shot up was now a ghost ship on four wheels, carrying no one but the dead to no destination at all. It slowed to a crawl, rolling slowly in a wide circle.

He approached the vehicle cautiously. Any one of the dead men might not actually be a corpse yet. Any of them could be shamming, lying in wait. He held the M-4 to his shoulder and checked first the back, then the front. Blood was everywhere. Every window had been shattered.

The engine was still running.

He looked back once more and saw the receding dust cloud. The Kawasaki had served him well, but it wouldn't put him in reach of his quarry. He opened each door and dragged the dead men from their seats, dumping them on the ground. Less weight meant more speed.

He climbed into the driver's seat, hit the gas and sent the Jeep speeding after the fleeing enemy.

Bolan drove so quickly that he nearly bounced against the roof. The powerful truck roared over the dirt road, eating up the terrain, achieving air as it roared over the larger dips. He urged it to go faster, ignoring the bone-crunching punishment he was taking, and the damage to the shocks and undercarriage. The vehicle had to last for only another mile or two. He just needed to get close enough to Nitzche to stop him.

Three Jeeps were left in the convoy. Bolan could see the rear of the closest one again. He was going to catch up.

There was an earsplitting peal of thunder. Bolan looked into the rearview mirror to find the top of the bunker was exploding, spewing black smoke and fire into the sky.

Grimaldi had gotten his shot.

"Hold on, Sarge," the pilot said through Bolan's transceiver. "I'm on my way!"

"Circle them and cut them off, Jack," Bolan said. "Blow them up if you have to, but try not to kill Nitzche. I want him alive so we can bring him back for trial."

"To make a point?" Grimaldi asked.

"Yeah," Bolan said. "A point about strength."

"You got it," his friend replied.

Bolan drew abreast of the last Jeep. The neo-Nazis inside cut loose with a fusillade that shot up the side of the soldier's ride. The tires blew. He struggled with the vehicle, trying to prevent it from flipping and crashing.

The Executioner shoved the muzzle of the carbine through the glassless windshield and pulled the trigger of his grenade launcher.

At that range the heat and concussion were enough to make him flinch. He peeled away, slowing his damaged vehicle, as the men in the one he'd targeted died fiery deaths. The noise of the Cobra attack helicopter roaring past above him was one of the most beautiful sounds Bolan had ever heard. He climbed from his dying truck and watched.

Grimaldi was finally free to put the Bell AH-1 through its paces. The Model 209 slid sideways through the sky as Jack fired up the M-28 turret in the Cobra's nose. Boasting an M-134 minigun and an M-129 40 mm grenade launcher, the turret was linked to four thousand rounds of 7.62 mm ammunition for the electric multibarrel cannon and three hundred grenades for the launcher. The hardpoints on either side of the chopper also mounted Hydra-70 2.75-inch rockets.

Bolan would bet even money that Nitzche was in the lead vehicle. Grimaldi obviously thought the same thing, for he avoided that Jeep while targeting the second with the M-134 minigun, strafing the roof. At four thousand rounds per minute, it took fractions of a second to rip open the truck like a tin can, turning the men inside to shredded meat. Bolan watched as the heavy 7.62 mm NATO rounds coated the Jeep's windows dark red from the inside before blowing them out.

The Cobra gained altitude, turned and ducked its nose, hot after the last fleeing vehicle. Bolan gave chase on foot, changing magazines in his carbine as he jogged.

Grimaldi used the grenade launcher, setting up an arc of explosions that cut across the road and forced the Jeep to swerve. The Stony Man pilot continued to harry it back and forth, firing into the edges of the dirt road with the minigun, showing the driver where the lines were drawn.

At any moment, with either his grenades or the rockets in the Cobra's pods, Grimaldi could erase that Jeep off the map. He was showing considerable restraint. Bolan very much wanted Nitzche back in a cell, to show that the American justice system *could* deal effectively with such a creature of hate. But he would settle for Nitzche's death if it meant the threat HN and Klaus Nitzche represented was ended for good.

The vehicle stopped. Playing chicken with a helicopter gunship evidently wasn't a game that Nitzche and his bodyguards thought they could win.

Grimaldi hovered. He fired a couple of warning shots from the M-134. This prompted the men in the Jeep to stick their arms out of the windows, casting aside their weapons.

Bolan shouldered his carbine and began walking toward the Jeep.

They had him. They had captured the bastard.

"Sarge, this is G-Force," Grimaldi said. "I'm getting a transmission from the Farm. The force of blacksuits they dispatched is on-site and mopping up. They're clearing the bunker, encountering minimal resistance. Barb reports that if any of Nitzche's HN types were still there, they were hiding or making their escape."

"The hostages?" Bolan asked.

"Safe. Except for Kinsey. Barb said he was DOA."

"Looked like a heart attack," Bolan reported. "He went down swinging, that's for sure. He was protecting the other hostages from Nitzche's bloody games when it took him."

"I'll relay to Barb," Grimaldi said. "She says Kinsey and Brognola were close."

"Yeah," Bolan replied. "Another good man lost."

"You okay, Sarge?" Grimaldi asked.

"I'm always okay," he said. "Cover me. I'm going for the Jeep."

"I'm your guardian angel," Grimaldi told him. Bolan could almost hear the tip of a hat in the veteran pilot's voice.

"You in the vehicles!" Bolan ordered. "Step out, one at a time! Driver first, then passenger, then rear seats. Nitzche, stay where you are!"

Bolan waited. The neo-Nazis appeared to comply. They climbed out of the Jeep, swaying in the blast of rotor wash from the chopper overhead, and arrayed themselves around the vehicle. Bolan didn't like it the moment he saw how they were standing. He went to a kneeling shooting position with his carbine.

"Don't try it!" he ordered.

They did, anyway. Each man was carrying a concealed handgun of some kind. They went for the weapons, which were thrust in their belts. Two of them got off shots that narrowly missed the soldier.

He stroked the trigger of the M-4. It was easy to ride the relatively light recoil of the weapon as he passed over each man with the red-dot optics. Wherever the circle alighted, someone died. He shot one man through the head, then another. The remaining two broke and ran.

"Leave me mine!" Bolan ordered. He pushed off and was running again.

In his peripheral vision, Bolan saw Grimaldi chase the other man with the chopper. This required very little effort on the pilot's part. When the neo-Nazi raised his .45 automatic pistol and triggered several rounds at the Cobra, Grimaldi squeezed a brief burst from the minigun. The dragon's tongue muzzle-blast burned brightly in the Kansas sky.

The neo-Nazi's head was vaporized.

Bolan shot his quarry through the leg, taking careful aim to make sure he hit nothing vital. Trick-shooting of that kind was always a risk, because you could never be absolutely certain of not tagging an artery. Bolan caught up with the downed man, took his gun and dragged him back to the Jeep, supporting him as they went. He threw the neo-Nazi to the ground near the rear of the vehicle.

Nitzche, frozen with fear, hadn't moved from his place in the backseat. That was good. Bolan wasn't interested in chasing the man down on foot.

"Hands where I can see them," Bolan ordered. "You and your man here are going to stand trial. Maybe they'll even let you bunk together...." He stopped talking. Something wasn't right.

He took a closer look at Klaus Nitzche.

The thing dressed in Nitzche's smoking jacket, wearing a slouch cap and matching scarf, wasn't a person at all. It was a mannequin.

The neo-Nazi on the ground started laughing.

"He outsmarted you," the man said. "He outsmarted you all! Heil Nitzche! You will never defeat us!"

"Where is he?" Bolan demanded.

"He was never here." The terrorist grinned. "It was a ruse, to draw you away while he escaped. You will never find him. He is long gone now, Jew-lover!"

Bolan drew his Desert Eagle and cocked the hammer.

"Enough," he warned.

To Grimaldi, he said, "Jack. Land. We've got work to do. I need a patch to the Farm. Whatever magic Bear and his people can work, we need them to do it. We've got to figure out what Nitzche's next move is before the trail goes completely cold."

"Coming in," Grimaldi replied.

11

"He was too young," Eli Berwald said.

Tears tracks marked his heavily lined face. He held the phone to his ear as if it were a snake, coiled to bite him. He couldn't bring himself to accept what he was being told.

"He was, sir," said Avi Kurz. A member of Aaron Berwald's commandos, Kurz had accompanied him on the raid of the Kansas bunker, where Lantern's intelligence indicated the old Nazi most assuredly would hide. They had been right about that. They had simply been wrong about everything else.

"Are you certain?" Eli asked.

"I am, sir. I was wounded. It took me some time to bind my wound, and then I lost consciousness in the trenches surrounding the bunker. We took heavy losses there, fighting Nitzche's men. When I came to, I was surrounded by the dead."

"I am so sorry, my boy," Berwald said. His voice was thick with emotion.

"It wasn't only our people," Kurz said. "It was also the HN fighters. In the trenches we encountered a government assassin named Cooper. Matthew Cooper, he said his name was."

"An assassin?"

"I don't know what else you would call him," Kurz said. "He was like the grim reaper. He killed so many. I have never seen anything like it. We were separated from him, and Nitzche's men attacked in force. We managed to eliminate many, but most of the team was killed there."

"What of Aaron?"

"Aaron survived the trench assault," Kurz said. "I found his body in the bunker. He was shot. The authorities were beginning to arrive. I had to escape the way I had come or risk being taken into custody. I regret that I couldn't bring Aaron's body with me, sir, nor look to the proper disposition of the rest of our team."

"No, no, you did the right thing," Berwald said. "Where are you now?"

"A motel in Kansas, sir. My leg…the wound is bad, sir. It may become infected. If I seek medical treatment, I may be arrested. It is a gunshot wound and will be reported."

"Do as you think best," Berwald said. "Perhaps you can tell them it was some sort of accident."

"I will try, sir,"

"This assassin, this Matthew Cooper," Berwald said. "Which government agency was he with?"

"He said the Justice Department, sir."

"Justice? Are you certain?"

"Yes, sir. I remember precisely, because I thought it odd, too."

"Very well. Godspeed, Avi."

"Thank you, sir."

Berwald hung up.

"I am concerned, Claire," he said.

"About what?" the woman asked.

"Avi's story sounds like, well, just that," he said. "A story. I'm concerned that Aaron's commandos weren't ready. They may have been physically prepared. Certainly they had the equipment. But they were untested in battle. We sent them straight into it. I'm concerned that emotionally, there was no way they could have coped. We sent them to their deaths."

He examined the carved head of his cane, which resembled a winged lion. The cane had been a gift from Aaron, made with his own hands. "What am I to do?" he asked. "I don't know if I can live with this guilt."

He stood with difficulty, leaning on his cane, and went to the window. Outside, the streets of Williamsburg, Virginia, were as busy as ever. From the top floor of Lantern's office building, the people below looked small, like children.

Like his son.

Eli Berwald wept.

Claire went to him then, holding him, her dark hair falling over his shoulder. "It is my fault," Berwald told her. He clung to the younger woman. "It is all my fault. My son has died because I couldn't save him, Claire."

"Aaron made his own decisions," she said, looking up into his face. "You could no more stop him than he could force you to do what you didn't truly wish to do. You are both so stubborn."

"Were," Berwald said, crying quietly. "Were."

"Come. Sit. I'll make coffee." She guided him to the sofa in his office and left him to his thoughts for the moment.

When he had come to the United States, it had all seemed so clear. America was the land of his freedom. When the American soldiers liberated Schlechterwald, he had looked on them as conquering heroes, practically gods among men. He knew how very close he and every survivor of the death camp had come to joining the facility's many victims. Nitzche, so young then, so brutal, so eager to kill, would gladly have executed them all, if only he'd had the time to do so. The Nazi's escape from the hands of the Allies had taken priority over revenge...and spite.

Spite. That's what it would have been. Revenge implied a

wrong, but the prisoners of Schlechterwald hadn't wronged Klaus Nitzche or the evil regime that had imprisoned Germany's Jews. And not just the Jews, but anyone Hitler saw as undesirable, any man, woman or child who could be sold to the Germany citizens as a common enemy. It was a brilliant strategy, really. It was brilliant in its simplicity. It was brilliant in its savagery.

Eli still remembered the look on his mother's face when she and his father had been separated from their son. "Orientation," the Nazi guards had called it. It had been some weeks before his fellow prisoners could bring themselves to explain to Eli what that word meant. At Schlechterwald, "Orientation" was the gas chamber. It meant a man, a woman or a child had been deemed so much useless garbage.

Garbage was disposed of.

Eli had vowed that no member of his family, no friend, no loved one, would ever again die at the hands of the hateful. He had built Lantern to achieve that goal. And he had succeeded! Or so he had thought, back then, when Aaron was alive. Then, when anything mattered.

Lantern could lobby the rich and powerful on behalf of Israel. Lantern could achieve results where lesser pressure groups failed. Lantern even funded several investigatory groups, whose task it was to hunt the escaped scions of the Nazi regime.

In the early years, there had been much of that. There were still many, then, who remembered the horrors of Hitler's war, of his atrocities, of his camps. Support for the cause of bringing these fugitives to justice was almost automatic. Men and women who grew up seeing pictures of the camps and their aftermath in newspapers and on television wouldn't shirk from the responsibility, even the pleasure, of taking final revenge on Hitler's monstrous children.

Time passed. Lantern grew more powerful, yes, but at a

price. Its workings became complex. Its lobbying became an intricate web of favors owed and favors given. It was now fully political. Lantern and its people, particularly its younger firebrands enamored of the idea of staging protests and even vigilante "raids" on enemy interests, were a force to be reckoned with, but every day, Eli Berwald felt his organization leaving its roots further behind.

Worse, around the world, anti-Semitism was on the rise. He had watched in dismay as Israel became further alienated from her allies. He had watched in fear as she had become the target of ever more hostile saber-rattling from her enemies.

War was coming.

He was convinced of it. War would come again, and the Jewish people would once again be forced to fight for their lives. Few were alive today to remember things like the Warsaw Ghetto Uprising or the camps themselves. The need to be armed, the need to be willing to fight back in the face of an enemy who wished to exterminate you, was a disconnected idea to most "modern" people, Jew and Gentile alike.

He was torn when Aaron came to him with his new ideas. Eli Berwald Sr. owned guns, yes. But he had nothing resembling the stockpiled armory, including even illegal automatic weapons, that Aaron proposed they amass.

The survival goods were for the most part things Eli hadn't considered, for he had grown accustomed to the luxury, the plenty, that living in the United States afforded him. The thought that it could all be swept away was an unsettling one, but nothing he couldn't comprehend. He had agreed readily to Aaron's plans to stockpile food, medical supplies, tools and other emergency goods.

He had resisted the weapons. It wasn't because he didn't feel they had a place. As things grew worse in the world, the idea of having arms on hand with which to defend his people became increasingly appealing. No, he had resisted because he knew what Aaron planned to do with them. Forming "commando" teams, militarizing the members of Lantern, training them to fight and to kill… Aaron was building a vigilante group, one that would make good on the many rumors already circulating about Lantern. It hadn't taken long for Aaron's leadership to permanently change their reputation. The organization was said to be hotheaded, with a penchant for vandalism and other acts in which they took to the streets to make justice for themselves.

That worried Eli Berwald.

He feared for his son and for what was coming, feared that such a commando group might one day be needed. He feared living in a world where that was so.

Now Aaron was dead. In death, he had proved that his own vision for the future had been terribly, lethally correct.

The courts had held Nitzche…and lost him. The evil Nazi commanded a private army on American soil. How could any individual man or woman stand against such a force? It would require an army of one's own. The commando force Aaron had been so passionate about building… Understanding this truth, Eli Berwald wept, both for his son's death and for the fact that he had argued with the young man so much about these matters.

Aaron had been right, and he had died proving it.

Berwald leaned heavily on his cane, going to the painting on the wall behind his desk. He slid it aside, dialed the electronic combination and opened the built-in wall safe. Inside, there were valuables and some documents. Most of the space, however, was devoted to automatic weapons: MP-5 submachine guns, purchased from improperly disposed government stock; Glock pistols issued to many government agents.

Washington, D.C., and its environs provided a wealth of ill-gotten plunder if one only knew where to look and whom to ask.

Claire returned, finally. She carried a tray with cups and accoutrements for Berwald's afternoon coffee.

"What are you doing?" she asked.

He looked at her bleakly. "I'm thinking dark thoughts about the war and Aaron's death." He closed the safe and replaced the painting. "I am thinking that I won't make the same mistakes twice." Carefully, he sat behind his desk.

Claire poured the coffee. Without prompting, she added cream and sugar to Berwald's, just as he liked it.

"You aren't telling me everything."

"I'm not," Berwald admitted. He looked at her. So young. So beautiful. "Do you know how long I have been creeping around the halls of power? How long I have lived a stone's throw from the seat of American government?"

"Many years," Claire said.

"Many years," Berwald repeated. "When you spend your time in Washington, talking to politicians, learning their strengths and weaknesses, you build a portfolio."

"Of contacts?" Claire asked.

"Of secrets," Berwald said. "This is a land of secrets. Secrets are power. Secrets point to power. And the man with the most secrets isn't the man most vulnerable, as one might think." He sipped his coffee. "If he has come by his secrets honestly, the man with the most of them has the most power."

"I don't understand what you're getting at," Claire said.

He regarded her for a moment. She had taken the news of Aaron's death surprisingly well. Avi had sent word ahead before placing the call to Lantern's offices from a location he deemed safe. Claire had shed tears for Aaron Berwald, yes, but then she had put them aside. She wouldn't let them hinder her. Eli admired that.

Now, more than ever, he needed that strength.

"It has long been said, here in Washington," Berwald said,

ignoring the irrelevant fact that Alexandria wasn't, in fact, D.C., "that there is one man in this city you don't cross."

"The President?"

"Let me tell you something about the President," Berwald said. "I have lived through the times of many leaders of the United States. Every one of them had in common the fact that he was more concerned about the consequences for him and his administration, politically and socially, than he was for truth or falsehood. A President is a curious creature, my dear. He wants to do right. He means very well. But it is my theory that no single human being can hold all the tasks, the work, the responsibilities of that position, within his brain."

"What do you mean?" Claire asked.

"I mean that a President is a creature of impossibilities," Berwald said. "Why do you think they all turn gray so fast? The office of the presidency ages a man because he is called on to do the impossible. He must live the lives of ten men, make decisions of twenty, accomplish his jobs in half the time it should take, and improve on the performance of his predecessor. No human could do all of that, and all the while, he takes the credit or the blame for a hundred different things over which he has little direct control."

Berwald managed to chuckle despite the ache in his soul. "No, my dear Claire. Not the President. Someone much, much more powerful."

"Who in Washington is more powerful than the President?"

"He is rumored to decide the fate of many," Berwald said. "A man who dictates life and death. A man who sits in an office on the Potomac and commands others. Those others, it is said, will go anywhere in the world, kill whoever must be killed, and disappear again as if they never were."

"You have been watching too much television again," Claire said. She disapproved of the late-night programming

Berwald indulged in, which she characterized as "conspiracy theories."

"It does sound fanciful, doesn't it? But for years I have heard it whispered. It is said that elements within our government command a vast network of resources. Men with special abilities. I know, I know. It is like something out of a spy movie. But consider, for example, the hijacking not so long ago. You remember all the fuss about pirates off the coast of Somalia?"

"I remember," Claire said. "There was the cruise ship whose crew and passengers were taken hostage."

"And sometimes, when that happens, you hear of elaborate military operations to correct the problem. Like the men who shot those pirates from the rolling deck of a smaller boat. They freed a ship captain who was ready to sacrifice his life for his crew. Think, Claire. How often do you hear something like that? Now compare that to how often you hear nothing at all. No story. No military tale. The problem simply…goes away. Why do you think that is?"

"I wouldn't have any notion," Claire said.

"The problem goes away," Berwald insisted, "because men who are specially trained in violence go to areas of the globe, or to places within our own country, and they quietly and discreetly kill everyone involved. How does one address a scenario like that? You have a boatful of pirates. You, let us say, board a Navy vessel, and you are trying to conceive of a plan in which you can free hostages aboard the ship without endangering their lives. A voice you have never heard calls you on your radio phone and tells you that the problem will go away. All you have to do is stay out of it. You are told to ask no questions. You are told that 'specialists' are on the case. And when it is all over and you are told that the problem is solved, you find dead bodies. Dead bodies killed in countless ways, all of them very efficient."

"What proof have you?" Claire pressed.

"There is no proof," Berwald said. "There has never been any, not that we can find. Imagine that. A powerful organization like Lantern, unable to pin down a single man who wields such power. It could be said such a man commands a private team of assassins. Such a man would have the ear of those in power, especially the President. Picture the job of the President as I have described it to you. So impossible. So fraught with pressure. Now you are told that for especially egregious problems, you may call on this man, this voice, and he will dispatch other men who will make your problem disappear. Because this man and the men he orders don't exist, you can't be held accountable. To the President, what could be more important? What could be more valuable than the ability to make problems vanish without consequence? Remember that it is consequence all presidents fear. The man who offers you solutions without consequence would become the most important individual in your universe. He would have power that trumps power. What would you do for such a man? What influence would you exert? What gratitude would you show him? It is unconscionable that any man should have such power. All of us in Washington whisper of it, but no one knows for certain. Never before have I spoken freely of it. Do not repeat to anyone what I have told you."

"Who?" Claire asks. "Who is it?"

"I have heard his name many times," Berwald said. "He is supposed to be a highly placed bureaucrat of the Justice Department. No one, especially the President, will admit that he is anything else. But so many politicians have said to me, 'There is one man in Washington I won't cross. That man is a Hal Brognola. "He is with the Justice Department, the same department that Avi says employs the assassin who abandoned my Aaron."

"Abandoned? You cannot think that."

"Can't I?" Berwald said. He looked into her eyes. "He kills like the grim reaper, Avi says. Yet Aaron is dead. Aaron, and not Klaus Nitzche, has left this world. What can this be except neglect, except indifference?"

"Then I will take my team," Claire said. "Aaron's commandos were our best, but my team, the second team, is also well trained. Aaron understood the need for redundant resources. He planned well. He has given us the instrument we require to make justice for him. Let me avenge him."

"You will," Berwald said. "My lovely Claire, you *will* avenge Aaron. But I won't send a child to face government assassins. You walk into a lion's den already, prepared to face Nitzche. I will not send you to a slaughterhouse."

"Then what?"

"I told you," Berwald said. "You don't walk the halls of power for as many years as I have without learning secrets. Some of these secrets are very useful, at times. Times such as now." He picked up his desk phone and dialed a number.

It took some time for the other party to come on the line. "The password," Berwald said, "is 'rose.' I am—"

"No," the voice said. "No names but one. The one that matters."

"Hal Brognola of the Justice Department."

There was a pause. "All right."

"It can be done?"

"It can be done."

"I want a message delivered," Berwald said. "Is this possible?"

"Pointless, but possible," the voice replied.

"Justice," Berwald said, "has a long memory."

"Very well," the voice stated. "The price will be high." The mysterious man cited a figure. It was a great deal, but nothing Berwald couldn't pay, and easily.

"Done," Berwald said.

"Time?"

"Immediately. As soon as possible."

"Immediately, then," the voice stated. He gave an account number. "Shall I repeat?"

"No," Berwald said. "I have it. I will transfer the money immediately."

The line went dead.

"Have you done what I think you have?" Claire asked.

"I have. Prepare your men. I will consult with the intelligence personnel downstairs. We will locate Nitzche, either by the internet chatter that so frequently gives him away, or through listings of his properties. We will find him. And then you will administer justice."

"Justice for my brother, Aaron."

"Justice for your brother," Berwald agreed. "Lovely Claire. I see so much of your mother in you when I look on you."

"Thank you, Father." Claire looked away. "I may pay the same price Aaron paid."

"If you do," Berwald said, "I will not be long after. We do what we must."

"And this Brognola? You really believe he had something to do with Aaron's death?"

"Lantern speaks truth to power," Berwald said. "There is no greater power broker in Washington—that has been rumored for years. I think it is time we spoke truth to this Hal Brognola. With bullets. I can neither forgive nor forget what he has done."

"Justice has a long memory," Claire said.

12

"He was too young," Hal Brognola said. He looked out the window, where the sunrise was an ominous shade of red against thick clouds. Predawn was giving way to another day in Wonderland. The big Fed imagined he could smell the corruption out there, as viscous as waste oil on the Potomac River.

"I know," Barbara Price said. She spoke to Brognola by secure satellite uplink, her image projected on the flat screen mounted on the wall of Brognola's Washington office.

"He was barely fifty," Brognola said, shaking his head. "I never thought I would outlive Lars Kinsey. Did you know much about him, Barb?"

"Only by reputation," Price replied. "He was the terror of high-profile criminal cases in D.C."

"Lars was the most courageous man I ever met," Brognola stated. "He never backed down from anything. When he started getting death threats, he began packing. He loved his Glock. They found it on the pavement after the first assassination attempt."

"Someone tried to kill him?"

"Yeah. Tried to run him down with a car. The work of a very high-profile crime boss facing trial none too soon after that. You may have seen the television movie after they put him away. He's still sitting in jail, thanks to a highly placed informant Lars convinced to testify."

"Shades of Striker's younger days," Price said.

"With less gunfire," Brognola said. "Lars walked away from that attempt, although I don't think his back was ever quite the same. He fought through the pain nonetheless. He never stopped working. He loved his job."

"I'm sorry for your loss, Hal," Price said.

"So many people," he stated. "We've lost so many. There are times when I wonder how Striker does it. We both know what he's been through."

"We do."

They were both silent for a moment. Finally, Brognola said, "Tell me about the bunker in Kansas."

"According to the preliminary reports and the hostages' debriefings, conducted on-site by our mop-up team, Nitzche escaped. The body count is high, most of it Nitzche's men. We've also recovered bodies who don't cross-check to Nitzche at all, several of whom can be traced to Berwald's Lantern."

"I knew it." Brognola shook his head again. "I knew they'd get mixed up in this. What's the damage?"

"I don't have confirmed figures yet," Price said, "but if they fielded a team in an attempt to take down Nitzche, they lost them all. And Hal, one of the dead is Eli Berwald Jr."

"Oh no," Brognola said, sitting up. "Does his father know yet?"

"We're not sure. The site wasn't exactly secure. There may have been survivors from Berwald's team. Striker reports that he is aware of none, but admits there's no way for him to tell."

"I suppose there wouldn't be," Brognola muttered. "What is the big guy's status?"

"He and Jack are en route by chopper. We have intercepted internet communications exchanged furiously between a man we believe to be Nitzche, or those working for him, and cells of HN stationed elsewhere in the United States."

"Cells? How many?"

"Undetermined," Price said, "but we are attempting to acquire a convoy of vans we think is headed for Williamsburg, Virginia. We're trying to use the satellites, but not knowing precisely where these people are, we've had to focus on their destination and work backward."

"Have you set up roadblocks?"

"We have a blacksuit contingent working with local law enforcement," Price said, "but we've had to keep it discreet. We don't want to cause a premature panic or tip off Nitzche's men. The roadblocks are disguised as sobriety checkpoints."

"What is the projected target in Williamsburg?" Brognola asked, fearing he knew the answer.

"What else?" Price said. "Nitzche's out for blood. He's headed straight for Lantern. He's rallied his troops and now he's on the warpath."

"What about alerting Lantern themselves?" Brognola asked. "Evacuating the office?"

"We tried that anonymously," Price said. "They thanked us very much for the information and then politely told us to go to hell. The police have had even less luck. They report, as relayed through my blacksuit spotters, that they showed up at the Lantern building and tried to hustle Berwald and his people out of there. They got no farther than the foyer. Seems Berwald has installed some pretty serious fortifications of his own. The police are holding on the street."

"Do they know a meat grinder's coming?"

"They do," Price said. "They're professionals. They'll do their best."

Brognola sighed. He removed a fresh cigar from the humidor on his desk and began chewing its tip. "This is going to get ugly," he said. "Keep me informed. I'll prepare to run

interference from this end, if it's required. I don't want a repeat of Berwald's interference with the courthouse mission.
I've placed a few calls to make sure that is well understood
by those who might be in positions to make trouble."

"There's one more thing, Hal."

"Yes?"

"Striker reports that Lars Kinsey died of a heart attack,"
Price said, "but before he did, he was doing his best to give
up his life in place of the other hostages. He was protecting
them, Hal, at risk to himself."

Brognola paused. "That was Lars. All that courage. He
would be the first to put himself on the line for a good cause
or a lost cause. It was one of the things I liked about him. He
always did what was right, even if it was going to cost him.
That's why he made so many criminal underworld enemies.
I'll bet there are more than a few who'll be crowing that he's
gone. People whose feet he held to the fire when he lived."

The big Fed laughed.

"Why's that funny, Hal?"

"Lars lived to piss those people off. He hated criminals,
hippies and politicians, in that order."

"So, naturally, he decided on a career in prosecutorial law
in Washington, D.C.," Price said.

Brognola laughed again. "That was Lars, too. He always
took the biggest bite out of any problem. Damn the torpe-
does and all that. I'm going to miss that man." He looked
down at his desk.

"What is it, Hal?"

"He was every one of us," Brognola said, glancing up at
the wall screen. "Any of us could go lights-out at any time.
A bullet. A heart attack. A freaking city bus. None of us
knows how much time we have. Riding a desk all these years
is going to kill me."

"You work too hard, Hal," Price said. "You always have. Get some rest."

"Rest, nothing. I'm making an appointment to get an assessment at the gym."

"Fair enough," Price said. "I'll update you as needed."

"And Barb?" Brognola said, before she could sign off.

"Yes, Hal?"

"You get some rest, too. Just because it doesn't show on that beautiful face doesn't mean you don't work too hard yourself."

"I hear you, Hal." She closed the connection.

Well. There it was.

Brognola had known for years that he was, quite possibly, working himself into an early grave. There were times while acting as director of the Sensitive Operations Group that he ate antacids like candy. During crises, he slept little. The bags under his eyes often had bags of their own.

When would his day come? He didn't want to consider it. But he wasn't taking care of himself; that much was true.

Then there was Barbara Price. She literally lived at the Farm, but spent far too much on duty. During emergencies involving Bolan or the other counterterrorists of the Sensitive Operations Group she would work for twenty-four hours straight or longer, trusting to the nuclear sludge Aaron "the Bear" Kurtzman called coffee to keep her going.

Then, of course, there was Bolan, who lived seemingly ever day before the barrel of a gun. How many times had the man been injured? How many times had he been shot or stabbed? How long could one man go on fighting?

They were sobering thoughts, and not thoughts for which Hal had answers.

All of them were mortal, and the fact was sobering. He lived, as did they all, as if he was going to carry on forever. Perhaps only Mack Bolan truly understood how to live one day at a time, and he spent his life throwing himself into the jaws of danger.

There was a knock on his door.

Roused from his reverie, Brognola stared in that direction. He checked his calendar; he had no appointments scheduled. He wondered briefly where his secretary had gone.

"Come in," he said.

The man who entered wore a dark, three-piece suit and carried himself like a bagman. Bolan had seen these middlemen types before; they scuttled when they walked, as if forever bearing the weight of others' decisions. Washington was full of them, all carrying water for somebody bigger, somebody more powerful. Individual bagmen like this might have multiple lesser functionaries downstream of them. It was how power worked in the white marble jungle.

"Can I help you?" Brognola asked. He remained behind his desk, well within reach of the buzzer that would summon security. While they were rare, the occasional crank or nut did get into the building now and again. So far, the security screening procedures at the lobby level had stopped anyone from getting through with a weapon, but Brognola wasn't about to get spit on or take a pie to the face, either. You never knew, in D.C., what a stranger might want of you.

"Mr. Brognola, my name is Simms," the man said. "I work in Oversight." He reached into his jacket. Brognola tensed. Simms's hand came back out holding a leather identification folder.

Simms's hands were thin and gaunt. He had high cheekbones, hollow cheeks and eyes that were bright and intelligent. He scanned the room, and Brognola, as if absorbing every last little detail.

Great, Brognola thought. Just what I need. An overempowered bean counter looking over my shoulder. Through the years, the black-bag operations of the Sensitive Operations Group had earned Brognola the attention of several auditors. In at least one case, they had even earned him a bribe attempt. He had managed to fend off all of them. The man who'd tried to bribe him, in particular, had gotten far more trouble than he'd expected.

Brognola was nobody's boy and didn't take to being treated with presumption or arrogance.

He took the identification now and looked it over, handed it back. The ID appeared real, but then, credentials passed out to the Farm's operatives like candy all looked real, too. Technically, he supposed those *were* real, because they were issued with the authority of the President. But if Simms wasn't who he claimed to be, Brognola assumed the little man would get around to explaining himself soon enough.

"Mr. Brognola, I'm here about a very sensitive issue," Simms said. "Does your department track...shall we say...the activities of certain problem solvers in the greater D.C. area?"

"Problem solvers," Brognola repeated. "I'm afraid you'll have to be more specific."

"I had hoped we could be delicate," Simms said, looking embarrassed. "I will be more direct. Mr. Brognola, you are a person of considerable influence. There are certain people who might benefit from you being removed from office. Does your department, or the agencies to which you are connected, track the activities of those who might be contracted to do the removals? People with power and influence. People who might be able to place such an operative in your proximity with a plausible excuse, supply him with appropriate papers and clear the way for him to...well, do what needs to be done."

"Assassins, you mean," Brognola said. "Hit men. You're wondering if the Justice Department has a line on any local wet-works specialists."

"Just so." Simms nodded.

"Why?" Brognola demanded.

"We have reason to believe someone wants you dead," Simms said. "We were wondering if you or, more importantly, your department had any knowledge of this."

"If my department had any details about an attempt on my life," Brognola said, "we'd probably be having this conversation on opposite sides of bulletproof glass."

"A fair point," Simms said, as he whipped a knife from his sleeve and lunged forward, intending to stab Brognola through the neck.

The big Fed leaned back, using the desk for protection. Simms went up and over it, incredibly agile, the black blade in his hand slashing the air.

Brognola had just enough time to hit the security buzzer before he was forced to abandon the desk entirely. The would-be killer scrambled after him, describing elaborate patterns in the air with his blade.

The .45 caliber Glock cleared leather, and Brognola got off a shot that punched into Simms's shoulder. The assassin fell back, dropping his blade. He scrambled up and, trailing blood, raced for the door to Brognola's office, the Fed in pursuit.

The gun boomed, but the bullet missed the assassin as he rushed through the doorway and into the corridor beyond.

The gunfire brought armed security men, already responding to the alert in Brognola's office, that much more quickly. They saw him, shouted to him and moved to intercept the wounded man Brognola was pursuing. The office building was large, and the big Fed's office was several floors up. Men and women dressed in suits and carrying briefcases scattered and screamed as the slight man with the wounded shoulder barreled past them.

"Hold still, you son of—" Brognola said through clenched teeth.

Suddenly, he felt himself being tackled. The guard bore him down to the floor, trying to pry the gun out of his hands.

"Not me, you idiot!" Brognola said. The guards hadn't understood, after all. They thought he was the shooter, because technically, he was. "Get off me before he circles back to us!"

But it was too late. Even as he said it, Brognola was aware of a presence above them. Simms produced another blade, ready to deliver a killing blow.

Brognola's gun hand was pinned beneath the security guard. He saw a second guard coming for them, saw the man begin to draw the pistol on his belt. The assassin saw it, too, and flipped the knife in his hand before hurling it with what appeared to be all his strength. The weapon spun and struck the guard in the face. Grabbing at his eye and screaming in pain, he fell to his knees.

A third knife appeared in the assassin's hand. Up close, Brognola realized what he was seeing. The blades were made of plastic, which was why the killer had thrown the last one so hard. They had almost no weight, and no metallic signature to set off the metal detectors in the lobby of the building.

Simms kicked the security guard in the head. The weight pinning Brognola's gun arm became heavier; the guard was out cold. Simms knelt over them and brought the knife up for a killing stab.

"Justice," he said, "has a long memory!"

"Glock has a short trigger pull," Brognola replied.

His own gun was pinned, but the one on the guard's hip wasn't. Brognola had drawn the weapon with his left hand and now pointed it at the killer. He fired off three rounds.

The gunshots echoed through the building, scattering bureaucrats. Simms collapsed on top of Brognola, his last breath rattling in his throat.

The big Fed lay there, staring at the ceiling. He still held the gun. He could hear urgent footfalls.

"Hal! Hal! Are you all right?" somebody called.

Then another security team arrived, come to save him at

ast. Brognola closed his eyes and wished he was anywhere
out Washington. His chest heaved.

Appointment at the gym, hell, he thought, struggling to
atch his breath. He was going to go eat a steak, have a drink
of Scotch and then take a nap.

13

"I see them," Grimaldi reported. "They're going straight for the roadblock. Sarge, they're not stopping!"

The line of cargo vans was traveling through the congested streets of Williamsburg. Grimaldi brought the chopper as low as he dared, but there was no clear shot, not while the vans moved in and out of civilian traffic as they were doing. The Stony Man pilot tried to radio ahead to the state troopers manning the "sobriety checkpoint," but there wasn't enough time. The first of the vans hit the flimsy wooden barricades and smashed them. The other vans followed in its wake.

"Jack, give me the law-enforcement officers and first response frequencies," Bolan said. "They may not be able to answer, but hopefully, they'll hear us."

Grimaldi made an adjustment on the retrofitted communications package in the Cobra. "You're go, Sarge."

"This is Federal Task One," Bolan said into his transceiver. "An armed force of hostiles led by escaped fugitive Klaus Nitzche is targeting an office building at—" He paused and checked his secure phone, reading off the address given in the Stony Man files for the Lantern offices. "These men are heavily armed and extremely dangerous. I am the leader of a Justice Department task force assigned to neutralize this threat. You will be advised of future developments as needed. Federal Task One, out."

Grimaldi switched off the link. "Think it will help, Sarge?"

"It might or it might not," Bolan said. "Come on, let's get in the fight."

"You read my mind," Grimaldi said. The Cobra dived sharply.

They came in as fast as Grimaldi dared push the chopper. The buildings to either side of the street, and the traffic below, made for tight quarters. They started taking ground fire as soon as they got near the building. Some of it was coming from the neo-Nazis in the vans. The rest was coming from the law-enforcement officers at the broken cordon.

"Well, that was helpful," Bolan said.

"Guess they don't listen too well," Grimaldi stated.

The vans were taking up positions to form a cordon of their own, blocking the front of the Lantern offices. From the building itself, gunfire erupted from T-shaped openings in metal shutters drawn across the windows.

"Sarge, do you see that?"

"Looks like Lantern knew something we didn't when they decided to stay put," Bolan said. "Can you target them from here?"

"Watch me."

The Stony Man pilot triggered the Cobra's minigun. Four thousand rounds per minute tore into one of the vans at the midpoint of Nitzche's column. The heavy 7.62 mm rounds tore the van open as if it were made of aluminum foil. The gas tank detonated and the entire vehicle went up in a gout of flame.

"I'll bet you a dollar you can't do that again," Bolan said.

Grimaldi whooped. The Cobra slid left and he very carefully tore open the next van in line. From the vans ahead of and behind the target vehicle, small-arms fire poured bullets in their direction. Grimaldi ignored it, although he did angle the chopper's nose up slightly. Both seats were armor plated, as were the engine and transmission covers of the aircraft.

The canopy, however, was Plexiglas, selected over armored glass for its lighter weight.

"They're moving," Grimaldi reported. "I've got a stream of them headed for the front entrance, probably barricaded against—"

The explosion from the front door of the Lantern offices produced a plume of black smoke.

"So much for that," Bolan said. "Looks like they've blown it. Keep on them, Jack."

"You want me to chance the rockets?"

"Too risky. We don't know how many people are inside the Lantern offices. We don't want to risk taking off the front of the building."

Grimaldi nodded. "I'd have argued with you if you said otherwise." He pushed the Cobra up slightly, then backed along the column of vehicles, tapping the minigun's trigger and alternating with grenades. The vans began exploding in sequence, but the process was too slow. The full destructive power of the Cobra still couldn't be unleashed. There were too many occupied buildings, too many civilian vehicles. Whether Nitzche knew he was using innocent people as human shields to protect against heavy weapons attack from above wasn't clear. If his actions weren't deliberate, the HN forces were certainly lucky.

"Put us down over there," Bolan said, pointing. "That parking lot. Time to get personal."

The Cobra didn't so much land as its rotors kissed the asphalt, giving Bolan enough time to hit the pavement and take to the street. Grimaldi lifted off just as quickly, withdrawing to take up a covering position. This time, there would be no choppering out of the target zone with an airborne bus full of hostages. Grimaldi and his electric cannon would be there to cut off Nitzche's escape route.

Bolan, rigged for full battle, made his way along the front

of the building. The burning vans now screened him from the street, which had been part of the plan. Denying Nitzche his most obvious means of extraction also protected civilians, cutting off the neo-Nazis from the rest of the area and obscuring visibility of the surrounding structures. The heat of the burning hulks made Bolan sweat as he moved toward the entrance.

Stony Man Farm had provided floor plans of the building itself, which he had studied in transit. According to the plans, there had once been a rear exit to the building. Satellite photo imagery showed that this egress had recently been bricked up. That fit with the relatively recent militarization of Lantern. Eliminating points of vulnerability, in the form of extraneous entrances and exits, was just basic security tactics.

It also meant that if Bolan was going to get into the building, he was going to have to do so where the HN forces had.

They had left plenty of men behind to guard the door. When they saw the soldier, they opened fire.

Bolan was getting tired of standing on the business end of Kalashnikov rifles.

Pieces of the building's facade were blasted apart as he ran, pelting him with sharp fragments of brick. The only cover to be had was a large metal trash receptacle set along the sidewalk against the building. He crouched behind it.

"Sarge?" Grimaldi asked in Bolan's ear. "You okay?"

"Temporary setback only," Bolan said. Not for the first time, he mentally thanked Gadgets Schwarz for designing the "smart" earbud headpieces, which filtered out noise above a certain decibel. When slaved to the communications link he shared with Grimaldi—and therefore with the Farm, through the pilot's commo package in the chopper—the tiny earbuds' relay prevented him from constantly broadcasting to Grimaldi and the Farm the deafening sound of incoming gunfire—not to mention his own shots.

The metal trash bin began to vibrate as the neo-Nazis concentrated their fire on it, but the bullets didn't penetrate the receptacle's heavy steel. Bolan considered his options, weighed the relative risks and decided that any nominal friendlies wouldn't be in the vicinity of the entrance as long as Nitzsche's people effectively controlled it.

That brought Bolan to the thorny issue of just who to consider "friendly." Lantern had, by rejecting the suggestion they evacuate the building, made their position obvious. They were going to stand against Nitzsche on their terms. Would they consider Bolan an enemy and shoot him on sight? It was possible. It was equally possible he would be shot simply by mistake, as relative amateurs under fire would be unlikely to discriminate when choosing targets. If there was any way possible, however, Bolan wouldn't shoot the men and women of Lantern. They weren't his enemies. They weren't predators. Foolhardy and untrained they might be, but their goals were self-preservation, not victimization.

The garbage bin continued to shudder. Bolan risked a glance past the edge of the steel enclosure. It was a straight run from his position to the doors. He just had to get past a wall of gunfire first.

A renewed salvo scored sparks from the top of the trash bin. Bolan pressed himself against it, trying to lower his profile further. Something was jabbing him in the back. He looked down.

The garbage bin was on wheels. Its foot brake had been gouging him in the spine. He looked left, then right, then removed several white phosphorous grenades from his war bag.

Popping the pins on the half-dozen grenades, he threw them into the garbage receptacle, then lowered his shoulder and slammed into the trash bin with all the strength he could manage.

The bin rolled. Bolan kept pushing, and it picked up speed.

When he reached what he judged its maximum, he let it go. The neo-Nazis continued to spray bullets at the bin, heedless of the danger as it bore down on them.

There was a tremendous crash as the metal garbage container struck the entrance. The white phosphorous grenades exploded a heartbeat later, bathing the front of the building in actinic glare.

Human torches ran shrieking from the site.

The neo-Nazis screamed as they went, blind and damned, their flesh alive with a fire that would gnaw through their bodies until the phosphorous was denied oxygen. Bolan brought the M-4 to his shoulder and quickly sighted, squeezing the trigger as his optics found their target. He shot each man through the skull, ending his screams, delivering final mercy.

Some men were evil, their souls blackened by a cancer that could only be burned away in cleansing fire.

Nitzche was one such man.

Bolan reached the entrance and took cover by the corner of the doors. Several corpses were scattered in the corridor beyond the burned, twisted metal that had been the security barrier. They wore black BDUs, in contrast to the camouflage fatigues of Nitzche's HN goons.

Lantern's people were already paying the price for standing against Nitzche's private army.

The foyer of the building was full of spent shells and smelled of soot. A stairwell led up to the next level; the elevator doors had been blown apart and empty shafts leading to the basement were visible beyond. Bolan cleared the space with his M-4 before judging it safe.

But it wasn't. They had been hiding in the stairwell above, waiting for him. When he paused to check his smartphone for the floor plans, they sighted from the next landing and opened fire, very nearly hitting him. The chatter of the Uzis in their fists was high and rapid. Micro-Uzis, Bolan thought. Their high cyclic rate of fire always gave them away.

The only cover, apart from bodies on the floor, was a reception and security desk. He dived behind it, feeling the bullets tear into it and gouge out chunks and splinters. The gunners emptied their weapons in series, staggering their reloads, giving Bolan no chance to counter. He lay as flat as he could as the tenuous cover of the desk was shattered piece by piece.

"Now! Do it now!" he heard one of the gunners say.

He heard the metallic spring of a grenade spoon releasing.

Bolan pushed himself up, popping from hiding like a jack-in-the-box. The grenade came sailing at him, as he expected it would.

He caught it.

As he snatched the grenade from the air, he was turning, spinning, and sending the bomb back the way it had come.

It hit the stairwell, then exploded.

The screams of his enemies were cut short as the fragmentation grenade blew them apart. Limbs and chunks of singed flesh splattered the stairwell.

Bolan's ears rang again. He vaulted the bullet-riddled desk and paused at the base of the stairwell. He could hear gunfire from somewhere distant in the building. Nitzche's forces were working their way upward. Berwald's offices were supposed to be near the top of the structure. If he and his people had made a stand there, they were trapped.

"Jack," Bolan said, "see if you can line up some more air support by way of transportation."

"You thinking roof evac, Sarge?"

"Exactly right."

"Please..." a woman's voice said. "Help..."

Bolan quickly scanned the bodies. Curled at the base of the stairwell was a woman in black BDUs and a Star of David necklace. Her face was bloody, and her stomach had been ripped open by gunfire. She was holding her guts in with her hands.

Bolan knelt by her.

"They're…moving up," she said. "Clearing the building. Eli and our forces are at the top. Can you…help?"

"That's what I'm here to do," Bolan said. "But how did you know I would?"

"You aren't like them," the woman said. "You are a soldier. It shows."

An alarm Klaxon began to sound. A recorded voice spoke with it. "Attention," it said. "Attention. All Lantern personnel. Flee the building. Failsafe plan. Execute failsafe plan."

"What is it?" Bolan asked. "What does it mean?"

"Nitzche's men have overrun our defenders at the halfway point," the woman said. "Aaron's plan was to evacuate if we couldn't stop them before then. He didn't want us…to be overrun." She coughed blood. "I was told…Aaron died."

"He fought bravely," Bolan said. "I was there when he died, too."

"How thoughtful…" she said. "Such a…handsome angel of death you make." She smiled up at him, her features twisted in pain.

Bolan bowed his head. The woman began to convulse then, and he held her as tightly as he dared. When the convulsion passed, she stared at him. Her eyes were badly bloodshot.

"It's too late, isn't it?" she asked.

Bolan paused, then nodded. "I'm sorry," he said. "I've seen it before."

"It hurts so much," she said. "Will it be over soon?"

He shook his head. "It may take a while."

"I can't stand the pain," she moaned. "Please. Please, help me."

"You know what you're asking?"

"Please," she said. "Don't make me suffer like this."

Bolan nodded again. He held her close for a moment, then lowered her gently to the floor as he knelt beside her. He drew the Beretta.

"What's your name?" he whispered.

"Madelaine," the woman said quietly.

"Close your eyes, Madelaine."

When she complied, Bolan squeezed her hand, then quickly ended her suffering.

14

Flanked by his men, Klaus Nitzche laughed with unbridled joy as he emptied his Luger pistol into the chest of one of Berwald's Lantern commandos. The young man screamed as the bullets tore into his flesh. The HN men flanking the old Nazi carried Kalashnikovs with bayonets affixed. They thrust their blades into the young man again and again.

Nitzche laughed again.

Glorious. It was glorious!

"They will pay! These pigs will all pay! We will gather the survivors and put them in camps! We will restore the glory of the Third Reich!"

He noticed the two HN men guarding him exchange glances, but he didn't care. They wouldn't understand. He didn't truly believe the things he was saying, but he wasn't mad. He was simply overwhelmed with the release, the purity of finally killing his enemies. To bring them pain, to bring them blood, to bring them death: that was what he desired most. Berwald and his fools had humiliated Klaus time and again. They had dragged him from the comfort of his redoubt in Argentina and made him live like an animal. They would have watched, gladly, as he was paraded for the television cameras, less than a man, less than a human being.

The ignominy of it. Jews and perverts and race mixers, subhumans all, standing in judgment of *him,* Klaus Nitzche, a man born to the Aryan race, a man who had once stood at the shoulders of the greatest leaders of mankind. How promising had been the Third Reich! How beautiful! He would never forgive those who had put him through a thousand and one disgraces as he clawed, fought, sneaked and ran to this pass. To crawl through tunnels like an animal, to hide himself and hope that decoys led his enemies away... This was the skulking of a rat, the behavior of lesser people. Not the strength of the superior race he represented.

And now they would all pay.

He reloaded his Luger and holstered it at his side. "Gun!" he roared. One of the neo-Nazis guarding him knew what he wanted and gave it to him. The HN trooper handed Nitzche a fully loaded Uzi. Its magazines were taped together, end for end, giving him double the firepower of a single stick.

The HN troopers were working methodically, brutally, from stairwell to stairwell, then fanning out to clear each room of the office complex. They moved like sharks, like wolves, like the hunters he had always molded them to be. The building was infested with Berwald's Lantern commandos. There were many more than his intelligence on the Berwald organization would have led him to believe. They were crafty. They had concealed their real numbers as they worked in secret to build up their forces. It was precisely what Nitzche had done in building HN, in safeguarding his person and his assets.

Even inferior Jews could recognize an intelligent idea when it served their interests.

He watched as a trio of his men with Kalashnikov rifles kicked down the next door in sequence. They were beyond the halfway mark now. Soon the building would be completely cleared, and they would leave. The police would have surrounded the structure by then, but of course, Klaus Nitzche knew something very special about this place that the authorities didn't know.

Such were the benefits of watching one's enemies closely.

His men had very specific orders. He waited for the gunfire from within the room to die down. When his operatives emerged, they gestured to him.

"We have three, sir," they reported.

"Excellent," Nitzche said. "With me." He swept into the room, the troopers falling in behind him with their Kalashnikovs ready.

Bodies littered the floor.

There were two men and a woman kneeling in the middle of the blood-soaked, shell-strewn linoleum. Their heads were bowed—their fingers laced behind their necks. One of Nitzche's men had remained in the room and held the Lantern prisoners at gunpoint.

Nitzche slung his Uzi over his shoulder with some difficulty. From inside his fatigues—he wore the same camouflage BDUs as the rest of his men now, but with his favorite black leather overcoat draped over his shoulders—he produced his pipe. One of the men offered him a match, which he took gratefully. He was only sorry Indio wouldn't be here to enjoy this.

"Four men, with me," he said. "The rest of you, continue the assault with the others. We will catch up."

"Yes, sir," his troops answered. They rushed to obey.

"Now then," Nitzche said. He reached out and put two gnarled fingers under the chin of the woman, lifting her head. She had very short hair, but was quite attractive. And young. That was good.

Nitzche strutted back and forth before the prisoners, enjoying his moment. The echoes of gunshots, of automatic blasts, of single bullets, reached them even here. The sounds of war brought back such treasured memories to Klaus Nitzche. He felt his eyes grow wet with the sentimental rush of it.

"Now, I will tell you something, my sweet little pigs," Nitzche said. "Do you know what I miss most about the old days? The days of Schlechterwald, when things made sense, and every one of you knew your place?"

When he reached for the woman again, she tried to pull away. He clenched his fingers on her jaw, surprised by his own strength, as he dug into the pressure points there. Her eyes shot open as he forced her to look up at him. He drew deep on his pipe and blew the smoke into her face.

"I miss," he said, "the decisions. Do you know, I used to end every day in Schlechterwald by forcing one of my guests to make a decision? It's liberating, my dear. You never know what you truly love, what you really value, until someone tells you that you must choose. Until life and death are all that separate you from the truth."

"What do you want from me?" she asked.

Nitzche smiled. "I want you to *choose,* my dear."

"Choose what?"

"One of these men will die," he said. He pointed with his pipe to the two male prisoners. They looked back at him in disbelief.

"What?"

"I said, I want you to choose," Nitzche rasped. From inside his pocket he withdrew an ancient, ivory-handled straight razor. Unfolding it with care, he moved to the first of the two men.

"Choose one," Nitzche ordered. "If you do not choose one, I will kill them both."

"You're insane!" the woman yelled. "I won't do it! I won't do it!"

"Oh, but you will," Nitzche said. "So many times I asked mothers to choose between their children, or fathers to choose between their children and their wives. I kept some of the results in my notebook. They are a fascinating window into human nature."

"No!" the woman repeated.

"If you don't," Nitzche said, "I will order my men to rape you repeatedly. And then I will still kill both these men while you watch. And finally, I will put a bullet through your brain. Now choose."

"No! No! No!" she yelled, defiant.

Nitzche growled. He drew his straight razor across the throat of the first man, then the second. Their blood sprayed bright and wet. He ignored their choked and garbled cries.

The woman was still screaming when he took his Uzi from his shoulder, cocked it and sprayed half a magazine into her face.

Nitzche was covered in blood.

"To me!" he snarled.

He hated it when they wouldn't choose.

He led his men back to the stairwell. The remainder of the floor had been cleared, or so he assumed. If it hadn't, he no longer cared. His good humor soured, Nitzche looked forward to taking his final revenge on Eli Berwald. But there was other, equally final business to attend to first.

With great difficulty, Nitzche ascended the stairs. His men helped him, practically carrying him as he neared the upper levels.

War and revenge were games for the young, it seemed.

"Sir." One of the troopers descending from above snapped to attention before him. "We have the last of the Jews barricaded on the topmost floor. There is a conference room one level below. Our agent waits for you there, per your instructions."

"Take me to him."

Under guard, Nitzche was led there. This space, too, had

been the scene of battle. There were shells here; there was much blood. Bullet holes marked the walls, the floors, the conference room table.

Seated at the table was one of Berwald's men.

"You wasted no time getting here, Mr. Kurz."

Avi Kurz looked up. "You instructed me to be on hand to assist as I could," he said.

"Hmm. Yes. Well, I see no reason I should expect you to do as I instruct."

"Sir?"

"Nothing. I suspect you wish to be paid."

"Yes, sir. If you wouldn't mind, sir."

"Very well. You know, they say the price of the Jew Jesus, of the Bible, was only thirty pieces of silver. Do you think your own ransom a bargain? I wonder what your fellow Jews would say if they knew you betrayed them simply for money. Fed us intelligence about Berwald's operation and the facilities here. Warned us that they knew where to find us in Kansas. Did they find it odd when you hung back during their raid, Mr. Kurz? When you, and you alone, survived?"

Kurz said nothing. His shame would be great. Traitors never slept easily, no matter how much money they had to soothe their guilty consciences.

"My money, Mr. Nitzche?" Kurz ventured.

"Of course," Nitzche said. "Of course. How easy it was to buy one of you. How little loyalty your Berwald and his progeny truly commanded. Were I he, it would make me sick, to think of how little it took to coax your betrayal from you."

Kurz stared at Nitzche but said nothing. It would be dawning on him now. They always understood, just before the end.

Nitzche nodded to his men. "Hold him!" he said.

"No!" Kurz screamed. "No!"

The HN troopers grabbed Kurz's arms. Nitzche held out his hand, and one of the men passed him a pair of handcuffs.

The old man clasped a cuff around Kurz's left wrist, snapping the other to one of the metal rings inset in the heavy conference table. There would be no breaking free unless the cuffs themselves were opened.

Nitzche removed the straight razor again. He placed it on the table. Silently, he stared at it, then at Kurz, then at the razor again.

One of his men took out a lighter and used it to set fire to the edge of an upholstered chair in the corner of the conference room.

"Our plan," Nitzche said, "was always to burn these Jews. If it cannot be the ovens, why, it will be their offices instead. And you may join them, Avi Kurz. The men and women you betrayed for so little. Or you may use my very own razor, which I leave to you. A gift."

Kurz stared up at Nitzche, pale with horror.

"An old man," Nitzche explained, "realizes he hasn't long before he leaves this world, and can take none of his precious things with him. And so I leave this to you. Look carefully at the handle, Jew. Look at the notches carved there. You will count thirty-seven. Thirty-seven of your kind died under that blade, at my hand, at my whim. Because I am Klaus Nitzche, and I am stronger."

He turned and left the room. His men followed.

As the conference room door closed behind them, Nitzche heard Kurz screaming over the crackling of the flames. Somewhere in the building, an alarm began to ring. He heard fire doors slamming closed.

"We have limited time now," Nitzche said. "Have you opened the access to the hidden elevator shaft?"

"We have, sir," answered his lieutenant, Max Rindle. Rindle wore a tool belt around his waist. He was Nitzche's preferred man when it came to matters mechanical. "It was exactly where the traitor, Kurz, said it would be. It isn't on the building plans. We've ripped open an access to the shaft and set up the drop line, as well as the padded harness to carry you to the lower level."

"Good," said Nitzche. "Help me with these stairs."

Beyond the regular fire door, the top floor was cut off from the lower levels by another steel security door, not unlike the one that had guarded the outside entrance. Nitzche waited impatiently as his men placed their charges on the hinges. He allowed Rindle to guide him to cover. Only after he had covered his ears with his trembling hands did he nod to Rindle.

"Do it," he said.

Rindle barked to his men. "Fire it!"

The explosion was deafening. It raised an ashen storm, choking them with hot smoke. When the cloud dissipated somewhat, the steel doors fell into the room beyond with a crash that vibrated the floorboards.

Nitzche could smell smoke drifting up from below. Soon the entire building would be wreathed in flame. Lantern would live up to its name, and it would burn brightly.

He was almost disappointed when the rooms proved nearly empty. His men swept through each of the offices, until finally they found themselves facing Eli Berwald. The old man sat behind his desk, holding a Walther P-38, a gun Nitzche well recognized.

"Drop the weapon!" Rindle ordered, training his Kalashnikov on Berwald. "Drop it now!"

Berwald made no attempt to raise the weapon. The P-38 rested on the desk, loosely gripped in the old man's right hand.

"We make quite a pair, don't we?" Nitzche said. He lowered himself carefully into the chair opposite Berwald, holding his Uzi against his body. "Do you know why I have come, Jew?"

"Revenge," Berwald said. "We sought to make you pay for your crimes. You wish to punish us."

"It is that, yes," Nitzche admitted. "But there is more. Do you know that I murdered your son?"

"Yes."

"And do you know that Lantern has fallen because one of your own betrayed you?"

Berwald was silent for some moments. Finally, he stared straight at Nitzche. "No," he said. "I didn't know."

"Ask me who," Klaus said.

"No."

"It was your dear friend Avi Kurz. It took only the promise of three hundred thousand dollars to make him betray you."

"You are insane, Klaus Nitzche," Berwald stated. "You always were insane. A man who delights in the suffering and death of his fellow human beings can be nothing else."

"But those I have killed weren't human beings at all," Nitzche said. "Why, many of them were Jews."

Berwald's eyes cut to Nitzche. The anger in them smoldered.

"Raise your weapon," Nitzche said. "Try to kill me. I would if our positions were reversed."

"'For the grave cannot praise you,'" said Berwald, quoting the book of Isaiah, "'death cannot sing your praise. Those who go down to the pit cannot hope for your faithfulness.'"

"How very poetic," Nitzche said.

Berwald whipped up the pistol and put it under his own chin. He started to pull the trigger—

Nitzche snatched it away. Berwald's face almost struck the surface of his own desk.

"No!" Nitzche shouted. "You will not rob me of what I have come here to take!" He stood, dropping the Uzi, clawing his Luger from its holster. The engraved weapon reflected the light from Berwald's desk lamp. Nitzche placed the barrel between the old man's eyes.

"Heil Hitler! Heil Nitzche! Heil Deutschland!" Nitzche shouted.

"One day, you will pay for what you have done," Eli Berwald predicted. "One day the angel of death will come for you."

Nitzche fired.

15

Something was wrong.

Bolan realized it as he worked his way up through the floors of the Lantern building. It was obvious, from the bodies, that he had missed the worst of the battle. He was encountering occasional knots of resistance from HN stragglers, but he wasn't seeing nearly the concentration of Lantern personnel he should be. If Berwald's people had expected to mount an effective resistance against a force as powerful as Nitzche's, they should have many more shooters. It was as if the majority of the force Bolan would expect to see had taken leave of the battle. But where had they gone?

The only option that seemed likely was the roof. "Striker to G-Force," Bolan called out. The tiny transceiver lodged in his ear carried his words to the Stony Man pilot. "Jack, what's the story at roof level?"

"Nothing, Striker," Grimaldi said. "But you've got a problem. The building is on fire. I'm notifying the DCFD, but it looks like it's moving pretty fast."

"I know," Bolan said. "I've been smelling the smoke. I can feel the heat through the ceiling. I think it's right above me."

"Can you get to the roof?"

"There's access via the stairwell," Bolan replied. "But I've got activity on the top floor. Nitzche and his men are up to something there. Stand by, Jack."

"Roger," Grimaldi said. "I am holding. We have a team of blacksuits cordoning the building at ground level, reinforcing the local police. I'm monitoring all the usual bands. Uh…Sarge?"

"Yeah?"

"Another possible problem. Among the vehicles at street level are a bunch of news vans. We didn't notice them coming in, but I'm watching footage of you entering the building. They don't have a close-up, of your face, but we're seeing you in profile. The story on Nitzche, his escape and the manhunt to recapture him is all over the news."

"Hal's not going to be thrilled. Good thing I'm not wearing my original face."

"Or even the one after that."

"Yeah," Bolan said. "Out."

The fire was roaring when he got to the penultimate floor of the office building. Ceiling sprinklers in the structure were going off, and Bolan realized the faint ringing he had been hearing was building alarms. Most of these appeared to have failed. The metal fire doors leading from the stairwell were hot to the touch as he passed them. Through a wire-reinforced glass viewing pane in the door, he saw a body on the floor of the blazing corridor. It was wearing a handcuff on one bloody stump of a wrist. The face itself was too charred to identify.

Bolan turned away.

When he got to the top floor, the fire door was blocked.

He tried to force it, and when that didn't work, he put his back into it. Straining, he realized that something physical had to be impeding him from the other side. There was no time to waste. He reached into his war bag for a plastic explosive charge.

There was none.

He'd run out. There was nothing to do now but improvise.

He jacked a 40 mm grenade into his carbine's launcher and retreated down the stairs, flinching from the heat.

He was going to be cut off if he stayed up here.

The grenade launcher thumped. The blast, in the confines of the stairwell, rocked him badly. When he shook his head to clear it, he saw debris scattered through the stairwell, and he heard nothing but ringing.

Bolan charged up the stairs anyway. He was lucky; the HN soldiers stationed on the top floor had been staggered by the blast. It wasn't until he was among them, moving the barrel of his carbine this way and that, trying to cover them all, that he saw the grenade.

He was still holding the carbine in front of his body when the concussion blasted him through the doorway to Berwald's office.

The world turned to shades of gray. Lying on his back, teetering on the edge of consciousness, Bolan could feel heat radiating from the floor. As he stared at the ceiling, tendrils of smoke drifted through the doorway, curling across the ceiling and collecting in the corners.

The soldier rolled to his stomach. The M-4 carbine was beneath him. Smoke rose from it, too. He turned it over and discovered that it had stopped several pieces of shrapnel that would have killed him, otherwise. He could feel himself bleeding from cuts to his chest, stomach and arms, but the wounds weren't serious. If he hadn't been holding the carbine when the explosion took him...

The M-4 was damaged beyond repair. He left it on the floor, to burn with the rest of the building. The smoke was now so thick it was choking him. He stood, supporting himself on Berwald's desk, and surveyed his surroundings.

Eli stared at him from behind the desk.

The elder Berwald had been shot in the head, squarely between the eyes. Despite that, his expression was in some ways peaceful. Bolan regretted the man's loss. He had chosen to walk the path of personal war and had died for it. No one was more responsible for Berwald's end than him. Yet there was no justice in a world where Eli Berwald died and Klaus Nitzche lived on.

Bolan staggered back in the direction of the stairs. The building would be engulfed in fire soon. He had to go.

The claw hammer almost took his face off.

The HN terrorist was bleeding from the ears. He had obviously taken worse from the explosion, or perhaps from Bolan's grenade to the fire door, than had Bolan himself. The man swung his hammer again, staggering as he did so, desperate to plant the sharp claw end in the soldier's skull.

Bolan dodged. He was still disoriented. The other man staggered as well.

The hammer whistled through the smoky air. Bolan dodged and slapped it away, moving to the outside. He threw a palm-heel into the neo-Nazi's face. The man backed off several steps, trying to keep to his feet.

Bolan felt his knees buckle. He folded against Berwald's desk again.

The neo-Nazi with the hammer collapsed on the floor nearby. He wore a holster, but it was empty, his gun lost.

The Executioner managed to draw the Beretta from his shoulder holster. He pointed it in the neo-Nazi's direction.

Around them, fire began to climb up the walls.

"My name," the neo-Nazi said, "is Rindle."

"Matthew Cooper," Bolan stated. "Justice Department. You're under arrest."

"Arrest?" Rindle managed to laugh. "You're no cop."

"No, but it's that or kill you."

"I doubt killing comes with difficulty to you," Rindle said. "But you will neither arrest me nor kill me. I'm already killed."

It was then that Bolan noticed the dark blot spreading across the stomach of Rindle's camouflage BDU blouse.

"Come on," Bolan said. "I'll get you out. Get you medical attention."

"The honorable killer," Rindle said with a sneer. "I've seen men like you before. Some even worked for that fool Nitzche."

Bolan eyed the neo-Nazi. "Sounds like you're not experiencing a high degree of job satisfaction."

"He left me to die," Rindle said. "I saw to his escape. He shot me to ensure my silence, when he had the opportunity. Nitzche has decided to disappear anew."

"How did he escape?" Bolan asked.

Rindle pointed out the doorway. "There was a concealed shaft added by the Berwalds. They dug a connecting tunnel to the sewer systems. It's how their forces evacuated when we overran them."

"How did you know about it?"

"A spy on the inside," Rindle said. "Easily bought. He died badly. Tell me something, assassin."

"I'm not an assassin," Bolan said.

"Yet you kill as others breathe," Rindle said. "I see the death on you. A man who kills, it clings to him. Like a smell, or an aura. Your aura is thick with the lives you have taken."

Bolan dragged himself to his feet. Flames licked at the walls and ceiling above both men. Black smoke roiled overhead. Bolan extended his hand to Rindle.

"Come with me," he said.

"Tell me something, assassin," Rindle repeated. "Why do you help the Jews?"

"They're people," Bolan replied. "Why do you help an aging Nazi murderer?"

"You know, assassin," Rindle said, "I think I would spend a long time asking myself that question—if I had a long time. There's one thing more."

"Yeah?" Bolan asked.

Rindle said nothing. He was staring into space.

He was dead.

Bolan left the dead, disillusioned thug to burn. He returned to the stairwell, retreating when flames burned higher and blasted up the stairs from below. Knowing he had only a few moments left, he leaped over the stairs to grab the ladder leading to the roof. Dragging himself hand over hand, he worked his way to the hatch.

Precious air flooded his lungs as he stuck his head through the opening. When he climbed up and through, rolling across the flat, gravel-covered roof of the building, the fire tried to catch him, reaching for him like a living thing.

He wasn't alone.

Several more neo-Nazis had gathered on the roof. They had no weapons that he could see, having lost them somehow, but they began to close on Bolan like wolves circling prey.

The soldier tried to reach for his weapons. His arms felt like lead. In the open air of the rooftop, he could feel blood soaking his leg underneath his blacksuit. He was bleeding freely from a wound he couldn't see. Limbs turning to rubber, he folded on himself, half lying, half sitting on the gravel.

"You're going to die, Jew-lover," one of the terrorists said.

Bolan snapped one numb leg out in a wide arc. He managed to catch the neo-Nazi and dump him to the rooftop. The others closed in. Bolan knew his only chance to prevent them from killing him was to go for his guns, but his arms wouldn't work. He could barely move his legs.

He was going to get stomped to death.

"Any last words?" one of the neo-Nazis asked, sneering.

"Yeah," said Bolan. "Jack. Open fire."

The hovering Cobra gunship unleashed a withering hellstorm from its minigun. The man closest to Bolan suddenly ceased to exist, blown apart by a hail of heavy slugs that seemed simply to wipe him from the world.

"Holy—" one of the terrorists said.

There was nothing holy about it. Grimaldi tracked each man in turn, using the electric minigun to turn the would-be killer to paste.

The last thing Bolan remembered, before waking up again, was Jack Grimaldi standing over him, saying something about a fire.

"Sarge! You with us?" Grimaldi asked him.

Bolan blinked. He had the disorienting feeling of time having passed, time he had lost. The Cobra gunship that had saved his life was parked on the pavement behind the two men. Bolan's head rested on a folded windbreaker. He recognized the jacket as Grimaldi's.

Across the parking lot, the Lantern building was burning to the ground. District of Columbia Fire Department trucks were pouring water on it. Emergency vehicles and what looked like the entire Metro police force had the area surrounded. Bolan saw blacksuits directing some of the cleanup and containment operations.

"I should have a punch card, as often as I patch you up between runs," Grimaldi said. "You were bleeding badly from a graze to the thigh. I taped it up for you. You've also got some painkillers and some stimulants running through you, courtesy of my little black bag of first-aid tricks."

"Thanks, Jack."

"You might have bled out, you know," Grimaldi said. "I'd catch hell if you did that."

"Sitrep," Bolan ordered.

"You're no fun at all when you wake up grumpy," Grimaldi groused. "There's bad news and good news. The bad news is that there's no sign of Nitzche. The building is a total loss, either from the firefight itself or deliberate arson. Doesn't much matter now."

"You said there was good news."

"Whatever escape route Nitzche used—" Grimaldi began.

"I've got a line on that," Bolan said. "It seems the Berwalds installed an access to the sewers. One of their own sold them out, so Nitzche knew about it going in, and planned ahead to use it as his exit route."

"I'll let Barb know, for whatever it's worth," Grimaldi said. "Our satellite picked up Nitzche on the way back out. He had SUVs stashed a couple of blocks over, planted ahead of time, we think. This was a well-planned op, all the way through. Come to think of it, this guy on the inside might have planted the trucks for him."

"I'd bet that," Bolan said.

"The Farm has traced Nitzche to a motel about fifty miles from here. The options are an overwhelming show of force, or—"

"Me," Bolan interrupted.

"Yeah," Grimaldi said. "Obviously Barb and the team would prefer you go in. There's less chance that Nitzche will see it coming if it's you, instead of the National Guard or a blacksuit force. He's a slippery bastard who plans ahead. As we've seen."

"Right. I hear a 'but' coming, Jack."

"But," said Grimaldi, "there's a complication."

"I'm listening."

"According to the Farm's satellite imagery, the remainder of Berwald's Lantern forces didn't leave the sewer. At least, not until *after* Nitzche and his men did."

"They hid out down there," Bolan guessed. "Waited for Nitzche to pass by. They either anticipated the possibility, or they were staged there awaiting the outcome of the battle.

Berwald might even have thought to hold them back as reinforcements."

"However it worked out," Grimaldi said, "we've tracked Nitzche leaving, and after him, a sizable force we believe is Lantern personnel. Thermal analysis tells us they're heavily armed."

"And?"

"They're tracking Nitzche, too," Grimaldi said. "Even if we muster a force, they're going to get there before we can."

"So no matter what, I'm walking into the tail end of a firefight."

"Looks that way," Grimaldi said.

"All right, Jack." Bolan stood, flexing, and began checking his equipment. The heat from the burning office building was perceptible even from across the lot where Grimaldi had landed. The fire was so hot, in fact, that the steel beams reinforcing the building's structure were twisting and collapsing in the blaze.

"Striker?" Grimaldi looked at Bolan questioningly.

"I'm good. Mount up. Let's go to work."

16

Claire Berwald fought hate.

It burned in the pit of her stomach. It traveled like fire up her arms, over her skin, into her brain. Hate grew inside her. Hate burned within her. Hate threatened to consume her.

One of the security measures her brother, Aaron, had instituted during his tenure as Lantern's director was to install hidden cameras throughout the building. Only he, her father and Claire had the receivers for the cameras. Using the portable video units, any of the three of them could monitor everything that happened in the building.

Claire Berwald had watched her father die.

He had tried to deny the old Nazi, Nitzche, his victory. Eli Berwald had tried to take his own life, to die on his terms. But Nitzche, that miserable bastard, had stolen even that. The sick war criminal would be satisfied only with murder, and murder at his hands.

She would show him.

For some reason she found herself thinking of her mother. Eli had met her later in his life, a woman much younger than he. At the time, their affair had been something of a scandal, judging from the genealogy materials Claire had seen so far. Old photo albums, and those old family trees, were all she had to remember her mother by, because the poor woman had died in childbirth. The loss had hit her father hard, but he had coped. For Claire, it only intensified the feelings of loyalty she had for her father and her older brother, and so she *hated* all the more.

The hatred for Nitzche, and all like him, threatened to burn her alive.

But she knew how to answer that hate. She knew what to do with it.

She was going to show them that she, too, could wage war.

With her were the remainder of Aaron's trained Lantern commandos, two dozen strong. It was more than enough for the combat operation they were about to mount. They had tracked Nitzche to the isolated motel, which squatted along a stretch of Route 64. Nitzche and his people had rented all the units in the west wing of the building. Their vehicles, and a few other customer trucks and cars, surrounded the motel.

Some distance away were a gas station, a convenience store and a trailer park. She had directed her commandos to converge on the motel using each of these as cover. They would attack from three directions, take Nitzche and his henchmen by surprise, and kill them in the cross fire.

Once Nitzche was dead, the souls of Aaron and Eli Berwald would finally know peace—and Claire just might be able to live with herself.

She keyed her walkie-talkie. "All elements, prepare to attack."

"Element One, ready."

"Element Two, ready."

"This is Element Three. Ready to go."

She smiled. Nitzche wasn't the only one who could train and equip a private army. Thanks to Aaron's foresight, her people had automatic MP-5 submachine guns, pistols and knives. They also had the training and the will to use them.

Nitzche was going to die by the sword.

"Attack!" she ordered. "Attack them! For Eli Berwald! For my brother! For Israel!"

From their disparate vantages, the attack elements opened fire. They targeted the windows of the motel. The strategy was to overwhelm the neo-Nazis with an initial assault, then move in to finish them personally. This had to be done with care, especially because they were operating in the presence of innocent people. She didn't want to risk harming anyone else who might be staying in the motel.

Claire extended the stock on her MP-5, chambered a round and brought the weapon to her shoulder. She sighted carefully and, as she had been taught to do, squeezed the trigger in short bursts, firing into the windows of the west wing. When she had emptied her magazine, she paused and assessed. There was no movement at the motel.

"Grenades!" she called into her radio. "Grenades, now!"

Elements Two and Three had 40 mm grenade launchers, purchased at great expense, or so Aaron had once explained to her, from a source with access to a National Guard armory. The thumps of the launchers were subtle, compared to the explosions that rocked the motel from without. Claire's people were careful not to walk the grenades in too deep. They didn't want to risk slaughtering people within the building who had nothing to do with the conflict. The grenades were meant simply to flush out their quarry.

Still, nothing happened.

She took the field glasses from her pack and put them to her eyes, focusing attentively. Scanning for movement, she still saw nothing, which was very strange. They had followed Nitzche to the motel. They *knew* he was in there.

"All elements," she said into her radio, "move in. Move in. Find them and take them out."

"Responding."

"Yes, ma'am."

"Roger."

They would need to work on radio discipline, she decided, but that was a problem for another time.

She walked in on the motel as stealthily as she could. The other combat elements did the same. All two dozen of her people surrounded the place, fingers on triggers, ready to kill, to avenge their fallen brothers and sisters.

Claire reached the door to the nearest motel room. She pressed her palm against it.

It opened at her touch.

Pulling a flashlight from her pocket, she shone it into the darkened corners of the room, careful to shift position each time she triggered the light. Still, nothing moved. She keyed her radio once more, turning to leave the room. "I think we've made a mistake," she said. "I think perhaps there's nobody—"

She tripped over someone's leg.

The man she had stumbled across sat up and grabbed her, clamping his hand over her mouth and slapping her rifle away. She tried to struggle, but he cuffed her violently several times, then slammed her head into the floor. She lost her radio. Then she felt his rough hands searching her pockets and fondling her body, taking her weapons.

Klaus Nitzche emerged from the darkness. "You poor, stupid little fool," he said quietly. "Did you really think we passed by you in your tunnels without noticing you? It was an obvious ploy. Baiting a trap for you was nothing. Nothing at all." He put his own radio to his lips. "Now," he said.

Automatic gunfire rolled over the motel like a thunderstorm. Claire's people fought back, but she could see the men from within the hotel rooms advancing on her people. They were caught in the open as they tried to close on the motel. Their only option was to retreat.

Go back, she urged them silently. Go back and live another day. We can regroup, even if you have to do it without me.

But then she realized they couldn't.

The SUVs were parked down the road, across the street and behind the motel building. Their engines came to life and their drivers piloted the vehicles to cut off the Lantern commandos' escape routes. As they closed in, their windows rolled down and the snouts of automatic weapons emerged from inside.

The sound was like nothing she had ever heard.

Engines roared. Men and women screamed. The automatic rifles sang out, breathing fire and death, spraying the interiors of the trucks and the pavement below with empty steel and brass casings.

Her people, caught in the cross fire between the motel and the gunmen in the SUVs, tried to run. They were cut down before they could get more than a few paces. Blood splashed the pavement of the parking lot. The SUVs moved closer still, forming a protective cordon around the building. The men inside them carried Kalashnikovs and wore the camouflage fatigues of Heil Nitzche.

"They are my reinforcements," Nitzche said. "The last of my reserves. We make our final stand here and now, eliminating you and the threat you represent. Never again will Lantern harass me. I killed your brother. I killed your father. And I will kill you…when I and my men have finished with you."

Claire bit the hand of the man holding her. When his grip loosened, she screamed, only to be silenced by another violent blow to the head.

"By all means, keep it up, Jewess," Nitzche said. "My men will beat you until your brains turn to jam. No one can help you. You are alone now. Well, you will be." He turned to his men. One of them wore blue epaulettes that marked him as some kind of leader.

"Morales," Nitzche snapped, "have the appropriate bribes been spread around?"

"*Sí,* my leader," the man said. His accent was thick. "We will not be bothered by the local police, as long as we clean up after ourselves."

"An equitable arrangement," Nitzche said. He looked to Claire again. "Make sure she watches."

With that, he stepped out, flanked by several of his HN troops. Morales said something in what she thought was Spanish to the man who held her. She was forced to the window.

To watch.

Nitzche moved slowly, as befitted his advanced age, but the prospect of cold-blooded murder seemed to put a bounce in his stride. As his soldiers guarded him, he walked unhurriedly from person to person. Many of the fallen Lantern commandos were still alive.

Nitzche murdered each in turn, shooting them in the head with his Luger. Every one of Claire's people who wasn't already dead met his or her end at the old Nazi's hands. Claire tried to turn away, tried to shield her eyes. The man holding her forced her head up and yanked back on her hair painfully until she opened her eyes again. Tears were streaming down her face, her chest heaving, as she sobbed quietly in witness to Nitzche's brutality.

He smelled of death when he reentered the room.

The Luger was still clutched in his gnarled hand. He holstered the pistol on his belt and smiled.

"So it was in Schlechterwald," he said proudly. "At my command, at my wish, they died. They died when I ordered it. They suffered when I dictated they should."

Claire made an elaborate production of throwing herself to the floor, weeping uncontrollably. The man holding her let her do it. Apparently such displays were acceptable to Nitzche. Perhaps he even considered a good bout of histrionic grief to be entertaining. The old Nazi was a monster, a sadist. She would debase herself in any way necessary to get to him.

"Please, Mr. Nitzche," she begged, tears dripping from her cheeks. "Please, don't kill me. I can be useful to you. I can make you…I can make you feel good. Please don't take my life. I'm much better to you and your men alive and capable of pleasing you…." She crawled to him as she said it. She moved slowly, on her hands and knees, stretching her body to emphasize her ample curves.

Nitzche was taken aback. He was, no doubt, fondly recalling all the prisoners he had abused and broken in Schlechterwald.

That's it, you son of a bitch, she thought. I'm weak. I'm nothing. Let me get close to you….

She began to crawl up his legs, pulling herself up by grabbing his coat. He was so amused by how degraded he thought she'd become that he let her do it. She kept up the act.

"I'll pleasure you as you've never been," she said. "Or perform before you. Please, please don't kill me. I don't want to die. Not like my father and my brother! Not like that! I'll do anything!"

"I'm going to enjoy," Nitzche whispered, "making you fulfill that promise."

Claire began kissing his chest, his neck, sliding her arms down his body until she hooked her arms around his waist.

She jerked the Luger pistol from Nitzche's holster, raised her arm and cracked him across the face with it, grabbing his clavicle and pulling him toward her in the same motion. Spinning the old man, she put the Luger to his head and hid behind him. The HN men in the room were dumbstruck. They stood where they were, paralyzed, afraid to move lest she murder their beloved leader.

Claire rammed the barrel of the Luger into Nitzche's ribs. "Out! Out the door!" She looked wild-eyed from man to man in the motel room. "Anyone who follows us will be responsible for killing him!"

Escaping the motel room wouldn't be enough. Nitzche's forces effectively possessed the entire motel property. She would need to escape the cordon. The only way to do that would be with the old man as a hostage.

She could feel the guns trained on her as she walked the old Nazi past the trucks. She wasn't sure where she was going to go; she just knew she needed to be anywhere but there. As she walked, she made the mistake of looking down, and saw the staring, dead eyes of the men and women she had called teammates only minutes before. She felt bile rising in her throat as she remembered the cruelty with which Nitzche had delivered the coup de grâce to each of them.

The trucks were her salvation. They were the way out. She jabbed Nitzche more forcefully with the gun and pushed him toward the nearest SUV. The man in the driver's seat was dressed as one of Nitzche's soldiers, in camouflage, with a pistol holstered at his side. He looked at her without expression as she guided the old man to the truck.

"Out," Claire ordered the driver. "Leave your weapon in the vehicle."

He removed his pistol from its holster, placed it on the center console and raised his arms to chest height as he left the truck. Claire stayed well away from him, mindful of tricks or sudden moves.

She prodded Nitzche into the vehicle. Then she strapped him into the passenger seat, using a pair of handcuffs she carried as part of her gear to secure him. Throwing the SUV into Drive, she gestured with the Luger, for the benefit of any of the HN men watching.

"I'll kill him if you follow," she called. "And when I do, it will be the easiest thing in the world."

She turned the SUV to the north, intending to take the highway back to civilization. She had just started to accelerate, however, when she saw similar black trucks moving in on her flanks.

"Your men don't listen very well," she said. "I'm going to have to shoot you now."

Nitzche gasped and clutched at his chest.

Claire looked at him curiously.

The old Nazi began wheezing. He started to convulse. The tendons in his hand stood out as he grabbed at his chest.

"No," Claire said. "Not like this. Not so fast. Don't you dare cheat me of justice, you miserable bastard." She looked again and no longer saw the other SUVs. Had it been her imagination? She didn't think so. But there was no sign of the trucks now.

Claire slowed. She didn't want Nitzche to get off so easily. After everyone who had suffered because of him, after the many horrible murders he had committed, dying of natural causes wasn't justice. Nitzche deserved to rot in a cell, or to be killed with the same violence he used on others. A brief bout of chest pain followed by oblivion would be an insult to every one of his victims.

"Don't you dare, you monster," she told him. "I will perform CPR on you if I have to in order to keep you alive."

Nitzche stopped moving. He was completely limp. He slumped in his seat, his face going slack.

Claire stopped the truck on the side of the highway. Keeping the Luger pistol pointed at Nitzche, she climbed out of her seat and moved over to examine him. She poked him. She prodded him. She even tried sticking a finger in his eye. He made no reaction.

"Damn it," she said. "No. It's not fair. It's not fair to anyone." She put her head to his chest, listening for a heartbeat.

Nitzche's arm came up, snaking around her neck, choking her, holding her fast. He pried the Luger from her grip and pushed the barrel of the gun up under her chin.

"Not so weak and enfeebled after all," he gritted into her ear. His tongue snaked in after his words, probing her ear, licking her cheek. She suppressed a wave of revulsion and tried not to move at all.

Through the windshield she could see the other trucks. They had reappeared after first disappearing into her blind spots. Armed men piled out of them, aiming their rifles and pistols at her, shouting, "Heil Nitzche! Heil Nitzche!"

"You little fool," Nitzche said. "Did you think I would be so moronic as to fail to post outlying scouts?" He laughed at her and then licked the side of her face again. "I have been four moves ahead of you since this little cat-and-mouse game began. You fools. You pitiful fools. I could have lived out the rest of my life in Argentina, and your father and brother could still be alive. But you had to 'hunt' me. You had to try to apply your pathetic notions of justice. The war was a *long* time ago. Had you left well enough alone, everything would be different."

"You don't deserve to die peacefully," Claire said, shuddering. "My father, my brother died trying to do the right thing. They died to punish you!"

"And yet it is I," Nitzche said, once more probing her ear with his cold tongue, "who will punish *you*."

17

"Are you sure about this, Sarge?" Grimaldi asked Bolan.

"No, not in the slightest. Just follow the plan and everything should work."

"Okay," Grimaldi said, sounding dubious. "You're the boss."

A high-altitude overflight in the Cobra, using the thermal imaging gear at their disposal, had shown Bolan what he expected to see: Nitzche was no slouch when it came to military planning. The engines of the SUVs parked at intervals around the motel were warm. The trucks were running, or had been recently, and they were there to run patrols, intercept intruders and catch stragglers. Bolan had come up against Nitzche enough times now to know what to look for. The layout at the motel was every bit the methodical—if improvised—fortification that Nitzche's previous encampments and redoubts had been.

The first thing Bolan had to do was take care of the outliers. He needed to draw the forward scouts away so he could deal with them. Eliminating them helped improve his overall odds, but more importantly, taking them out of the equation left him free to run the rest of his operation to penetrate and overwhelm Nitzche's encampment from within.

Real-time satellite imaging from the Farm had also told Bolan and Grimaldi that Nitzche had already fended off one attack this night. The number of bodies involved revealed that the last remnant of Lantern had made itself known, and just as quickly died trying. At least, Bolan thought cynically, this initial skirmish would have depleted some of Nitzche's reserves of ammo while dulling his troops' edge, even if they remained well equipped and well armed after the onslaught.

The thermal reconnaissance of the camp, now that night had fallen, also told Bolan exactly where he needed to be, and provided him with the necessary cover to get there. Grimaldi conveyed him to a point far enough away that the outlying scouts wouldn't hear the chopper land, or at least not be able to place the sound. He was, according to the coordinates now locked into his phone, within twenty minutes' brisk run of the first of the forward trucks.

"Wait for my signal," Bolan told Grimaldi. "Then you know what to do."

"Sure thing, Sarge," the Stony Man pilot said. "Good hunting." The Cobra lifted off again, leaving Bolan to do what he did best: fight evil while moving forward.

Dressed in his blacksuit, with his face smeared with combat cosmetics, and carrying a chest-slung mini-Uzi submachine gun from the cache of weapons in the Cobra, Bolan was ready for a night op. He jogged to within striking distance of the first outlying truck. Crouching, he let the night sky—naturally lighter than the terrain below it—silhouette the truck for him. Then he crawled toward it.

Three men sat in the SUV talking about whatever it was that neo-Nazis chatted about. Their windows were down and they were smoking. Poor discipline with this lot, Bolan reflected. Always poor discipline.

He drew his combat dagger and crept up to the side of the SUV, waiting for the man smoking in the passenger seat to extend his arm out the window. When the neo-Nazi went to flick the ash from his cigarette, Bolan reached up with his free hand, wrapped his fingers around the man's wrist and pulled sharply.

The man wasn't pulled from the window, but he shifted in his seat, his armpit coming up and over the sill of the door. Bolan rammed the knife into the gap, yanked it out and rammed it in again.

The SUV's engine came to life. The Executioner popped up on the passenger side, slipped his Beretta from its holster and drilled a suppressed 9 mm round through the head of the driver, coring his skull through from ear to ear. The man in the backseat had time to open his mouth to scream. Bolan put a bullet through it.

Taking a moment to dump the bodies, Bolan jumped behind the wheel of the SUV, then consulted the coordinates he and Grimaldi had plotted in his phone. There were two more outlier trucks. When he was finished with those vehicles, he would penetrate the enemy cordon around the motel.

Simple.

Throwing the SUV into gear, he stomped on the gas pedal and sent the stolen, bullet-pocked vehicle speeding through the darkness. Keeping the motel between his position and the third truck, he targeted the second. He rolled up on it casually, as if just stopping by for a chat, parking the vehicle next to but slightly behind the other SUV. Then he got out.

He was holding a pair of white phosphorous grenades in his hands.

Expression grim, Bolan popped the pins on the Willie Pete grenades, let the spoons fly free and ran for the SUV. These men, too, were seated with their windows open, and Bolan simply ran past and dumped the grenades into the truck. When he had achieved what he thought was safe distance, he went prone.

The flash lit the night sky and produced a bloodcurdling trio of screams from the men in the suddenly burning SUV.

White fire crawled over their bodies, turning them into blackened, cooked husks. The tendrils of stark white brilliance climbed into the blackness, producing enough heat that Bolan could only drive past, check and back off again.

Two down.

The third would be the easiest, because for it, he had no intention of sparing his vehicle. He put the accelerator to the floor and guided the truck around the motel, changing his angle until he was on a collision course with truck number three.

As he neared, he saw he'd lucked into another fortunate circumstance: one of the men in the SUV had gotten out of the vehicle to relieve himself. Bolan poured on the power. The grille of the SUV struck the neo-Nazi, grinding the screaming man under the front bumper of the truck. Bolan paused long enough to make sure the guy was dead, then hit the accelerator again and rammed the third truck.

As the two vehicles collided, he raised his mini-Uzi and hosed down the windows. The 9 mm bullets chewed through the two men still inside, spreading them over the dash, the seats and even the roof.

Bolan climbed out and surveyed his work.

So much for the forward guard.

He turned and ran toward the cordon of vehicles around the motel. There was no police response to all the destruction. The longer that went on, Bolan figured, the greater were the chances that Nitzche had bribed or otherwise influenced the relevant local law-enforcement concerns.

The sounds of battle had drawn out many of Nitzche's men. They stood ready behind the cordon of their vehicles, Kalashnikovs and other automatic weapons at the ready. Bolan decided he would see just how many he could draw away from the improvised battlements. He lay flat in the darkness and made a variety of clicking noises, imitating a battery-powered radio. Several of the neo-Nazis peeled off from the main contingent, holding flashlights cautiously before them.

He didn't use his guns. Instead, he worked his way through the terrorists using his knife, quietly and efficiently killing each man. It wasn't long before the tactic had the desired effect. The neo-Nazis began to freak out and call to one another, trying to determine what was going on.

"My leg! My leg!" Bolan cried in a high-pitched voice. "Oh God!"

"Who's out there?" demanded one HN guard. "Show yourself!"

"We should all just kill ourselves now!" Bolan yelled.

"There's got to be a full squad out there!" one of the terrorists shouted to his fellows.

It was time. The soldier picked his way through their lines, using their frightened voices to fix them in the night. Then he came up behind one and, grabbing the neo-Nazi around the mouth, stabbed him to death with the combat dagger.

Skulking among the enemy, Bolan continued attacking them silently, from behind their line. When they finally caught on, they began screaming to one another in renewed fear. A predator was loose in their midst, and for once, none of the neo-Nazis were themselves that predator. They were instead the prey, a role that came none too easily to such brutal, simple men.

Bolan picked up his pace. He ran back and forth among the neo-Nazis, skirting the fronts of the motel doors, weaving in and out of the parked SUVs. His knives found their mark wherever he went, rending and tearing, stabbing and cleaving. Finally, perhaps on an order from Klaus Nitzche himself, the remaining neo-Nazis rallied and pulled portable spotlights from their vehicles. The handheld light guns were of the type that plug into a vehicle's cigarette lighter, producing bright beams of white light.

Bolan was caught in the glare.

"There!" somebody shouted. "That's him! Kill him, kill him!"

"No!" The order came from Nitzche, closer than Bolan had thought the old Nazi would be. "You have him now! Take him alive! Move in, move in! I want him groveling before me!"

A lack of discipline, Bolan thought, and an overabundance of pride. Incompetence and overconfidence killed more of his foes than his bullets ever could.

Bolan stopped moving. He let the neo-Nazis come, moving to surround him, creeping ever closer. They were truly in fear of him now. They had seen how many of their number he had killed with only a knife. The big combat dagger dripped blood, which was visible in the bright lights from the vehicles.

Wait for it, Bolan thought.

"Now, Sarge?" Grimaldi asked in his ear.

"Not yet," he whispered.

Nitzche left his motel room. He held his Luger in his hand again and seemed intent on using it. Bolan let him come. The sound of the Cobra gunship was now just perceptible to those on ground. A slight breeze kicked up by the rotor blades blew grit against Bolan's feet.

"So," Nitzche said. "The mighty Matthew Cooper of the United States government. How did you find me, Cooper?"

"The same way Lantern did," Bolan said.

"Like lambs to slaughter, I led them to me," Nitzche crowed. "Are you now to follow them? Honestly, Cooper, I had thought the resistance you offered me would be so much greater. At every turn, my vast superiority has been proved by—"

"A lack of discipline," Bolan said, "and an overabundance of pride."

"What?" Nitzche said. He peered at Bolan, suspicious. "What do you mean?"

"Reaper," the Executioner said.

The first SUV in the cordon exploded.

The Cobra gunship floated overhead. Grimaldi operated the minigun like a surgeon, destroying each truck in succession, creating a raging ring of fire around the motel. When he had finished strafing the trucks with the electric cannon, the Stony Man pilot began firing incendiary grenades. The circle of fire grew higher and hotter, burning with an intensity that threatened to scorch the paint from the walls of the motel.

Hell had come to Klaus Nitzche's doorstep.

The neo-Nazis were now trapped within the ring of fire. Bolan went to work with his Uzi, firing on full automatic, running to and fro among the flames, blasting each man he acquired. Screams filled the air once more. Bolan began throwing open the doors of the motel room's west wing, the area protected by the now-burning cordon. He cleared room after room, emptying the Uzi and all his spare magazines for it, discarding the weapon when it was no longer useful.

A pistol in each hand, Bolan continued shooting. The neo-Nazis who tried to engage him fell before his guns. Whether hiding behind cover or rushing him in the open, they had no chance. Bolan was an avenging fury.

He emptied his pistols, reloaded, fired again. Over and over again, he blasted the weapons dry, until the barrels of both pistols were burning hot and he had depleted all the rounds he carried with him. With every step he took, he walked on empty shell casings and through puddles of blood. The Executioner had created a killing ground penned in by fire and drenched in fear. For the Heil Nitzche fighters, it truly was hell on earth.

And then they were all dead.

Bolan stood, breathing heavily. His weapons were too hot to holster. He placed them, and his war bag, on the blood-soaked pavement. Bending to pick up a revolver from a dead man's hand, he opened the cylinder and checked the cartridges. The man hadn't gotten off a single shot. Bolan closed the weapon and, gun in hand, went for the only door that was still closed. It was the last motel room. Nitzche would be hiding there. He would be cowering, having retreated during the furious carnage Bolan had just wrought.

He would die.

Bolan didn't knock. He kicked the door open and then pressed himself against the doorjamb as bullets burned the air where he had been. He answered the shots with his revolver, dropping the neo-Nazis where they stood. When the gun was empty, he threw it aside.

Only Nitzche remained.

The aged Nazi held his Luger under Claire Berwald's chin. "You remember the young lady?" Nitzche growled. "Or have you two not yet met? There are so many of these Berwalds, it seems. It is hard to keep track."

"I haven't really had the pleasure," Bolan said. "Not properly."

"I have." Nitzche smiled lasciviously. "Or at least, I have *started* to. When you are dead, I will leave this place and make her suffer a thousand humiliations before I finally kill her. She will go to her dead father and brother a broken woman."

Bolan's jaw tightened. "You really are an evil piece of filth," he said, drawing his knife.

"You *dare?*" Nitzche snarled. "Perhaps I will kill her right now."

"She's the only thing keeping you alive," Bolan said.

"Damn you. Damn you!"

Claire rammed her elbow up into the hollow of Nitzche's throat. The old Nazi's head snapped back and he made a horrible choking noise. He began to crumple.

Claire leaped out of the line of fire. Bolan reversed his

blade and flipped it, end for end, with all his strength. The razor-sharp knife bit deep, burying itself in Nitzche's neck. Blood sprayed everywhere. The old man sank to the floor, clawing at the hilt of the knife jutting from his throat, rolling back and forth. He was saying something, screaming something, but his words were unintelligible, given the blood roiling in his throat.

Claire Berwald made a soft noise. Her eyes began to roll up in her head.

Bolan grabbed her before she fell. He pulled her to him, held her close, as the adrenaline dump hit her hard, causing her to shake as if she were having a seizure.

"Claire," Bolan said. "Claire! Stay with me! It's shock. You're all right. You're going to be all right."

She looked up at him. "You…saved my life. Freed me."

He reached into his pocket and produced the ring Aaron Berwald had given him. "Your brother wanted you to have this. I was with him…at the end."

Claire looked down at the ring. "You tried to help him?"

"I did everything I could," Bolan said. "It wasn't enough."

"Sometimes," she murmured, "it isn't." She looked at the dead bodies everywhere. "This place is a charnel house."

"My people will see to it," Bolan told her.

He put two fingers to his ear for her benefit. "Jack," he said, "call our mutual friends. Have them send a cleanup crew to this location. There's one hell of a mess down here."

"You got it," Grimaldi said.

"You are…?" Claire looked at the soldier, confused.

"Matthew Cooper. I'm with the Justice Department. When Nitzche first took the courthouse, I was assigned to intercede. I've been pursuing him ever since."

As if remembering the evil Nazi, Claire turned and stared. Nitzche was still writhing on the floor, bleeding out. His movements were becoming weaker.

"He's still alive," she said, her voice full of wonder. "How can a man live through that?"

"He can't," Bolan said. "Not this one." He leaned down and, making eye contact with Nitzche, wrapped his fingers around the hilt of the big knife. "I want you to know something," he told him. The Nazi's eyes were wide with outrage. He was pale and cold. He didn't have long.

"When you get to hell," Bolan told Nitzche, "I want you to know it was a Jew-lover who sent you there. A man who believes in everything you despise. A man who thinks there is no lower human being on this earth than a Nazi...unless it is the neo-Nazis who follow him. Go to hell, Klaus Nitzche, and may your suffering be as dishonorable and unclean as your death."

Bolan wrenched the knife back and forth, then removed it.

Nitzche died staring toward the ceiling, surrounded by a spreading pool of his own blood.

Claire turned away. Bolan stood. He started for the exit.

The door to the connecting room opened.

Indio, Nitzche's Uruguayan lieutenant, stood there.

"None of us is leaving here alive," the giant told them.

18

The giant had a large bandage over his forehead. He pointed at the bloody gauze. "You shot me in the head," he said. "But on the streets of Buenos Aires I was once struck in the skull with a steel pipe. I might have died. Instead, I was given a metal plate."

Indio gestured for the door. "The parking lot," he said. "I will fight you, government man. You have killed my leader, and for that I will make you suffer greatly. But unlike my leader, I respect my enemies when they prove worthy. You are a very worthy fighter. I have always enjoyed combat. This will be very good indeed."

"You don't seem too broken up about Nitzche," Bolan observed.

"I was not so blindly loyal as he thought," Indio said, "nor as simpleminded. Perhaps I will take the reins of Heil Nitzche. Perhaps he will become a symbol, a beloved martyr, better remembered than obeyed."

"I doubt it," Bolan said.

"I doubt it, too," Indio agreed. "I have no desire to go to prison. But soon this place will be overrun with police, and I will have no choice. I would rather die on my feet. If there's time, I will rape the woman until she begs me to kill her, too." He drew a large bowie knife from his belt. "And I would like to very much to stab you to death."

"Well," Bolan said, "let's do it."

Indio charged; Bolan dodged the knife. He hit the door and ran for the parking lot, drawing Indio away from Claire before the giant got any ideas. The two squared off outside, in the shadows of the smoldering trucks. Indio stepped in, slashing and stabbing.

Bolan knew there was a very good chance Indio was more skilled in this particular method of combat. He focused only on the most basic elements, remembering all his training, all his experience. To fight a man with a knife was one of the most dangerous things a human could do. Indio was intent on killing him, and should he succeed, Claire would suffer a horrible, painful death by sexual torture.

Bolan stood with his arms out at his sides, making sure his limbs weren't within the "barrel," the area in which an enemy knife could strike. Indio advanced, cutting and slashing widely. Bolan dodged, using his footwork and his body positioning to keep him out of danger.

This tactic soon began to frustrate Indio. The scars along his left forearm told the tale. The giant was accustomed to "stand up" knife fights in which the combatants traded blows and cut each other. Doubtless, his sheer size was an advantage in such a war of bloody attrition, for Indio could afford to take knife wounds that would kill a smaller, lighter man.

Back and forth they fought. Each time Indio came in for a pass, he was closer to scoring a deadly blow. Bolan realized he was tiring, and when his strength finally gave out, the Uruguayan would win. The knife was deadly precisely because it required very little skill or strength to operate. All Bolan had to do was screw up badly enough and he would die. It wouldn't take much on Indio's part to manage it.

"Why are you afraid?" Bolan asked. It was a dangerous gambit, but it was all he had.

"I'm not afraid of you!" Indio insisted.

"You begged Nitzche to let you kill me," Bolan said.

"Yes," Indio replied. "It would have been better for him."

"But that was *your* fear talking, Indio," Bolan taunted. "Nitzche was unafraid."

"He was frequently reckless."

"Face me like a man," Bolan said. "Face me without a weapon." He sheathed his knife.

Indio smiled. He threw his bowie knife aside. "I will show you," he stated. "I will show you why so many fear *me*." He advanced; Bolan backed away. The two men started circling each other, stepping over bodies and debris in the parking lot. Indio was flexing his fingers, clearly picturing getting his enormous hands on Bolan and rending him limb from limb. Only the giant's ego gave Bolan any advantage. Indio was, for all his strength, insecure about his abilities, forever concerned about proving himself.

The Uruguayan tried to shoot in for a takedown several times. In all cases, Bolan avoided it. The soldier was leading Indio farther and farther from the motel, through the parking lot, away from Claire. He led the big man past the cordon of smoking trucks and farther still. Finally, he was satisfied with their position, and looked at his opponent.

"I'm not actually interested in fighting you, Indio."

"But I very much wish to fight you. You do not have to fight back. I can simply kill you, if you wish it to be quick." Indio shot in again, and this time succeeded in taking Bolan to the ground, knocking the breath out of the soldier.

Indio went to punch Bolan from the mount position. Were he to land a blow to the body like that, he might quite possibly pulp one or more of Bolan's organs. The soldier was ready for that and managed to shift to the side. Indio struck the pavement instead. He roared in pain. Wrapping his fingers around Bolan's throat, he went for the choke. The soldier hammered away at Indio's elbows with the edges of his hands and managed to dislodge the giant's arms.

"You offer much more sport than my usual wrestling partners." Indio grinned. "Do you know what I enjoy most about raping a woman?"

"Not interested," said Bolan, who could feel his ribs being crushed.

"I enjoy her hope," Indio stated. "Her belief that perhaps she will escape. There's nothing like taking a woman who doesn't believe such a thing could happen to her, who thinks that surely help will come at the last moment. The light dies in their eyes when they realize it is going to happen, it is happening, it has happened, and nothing for them will ever be the same again."

"Killing you," Bolan said, "will be doing the world a great favor."

"Perhaps," Indio admitted.

"Will you indulge a dying man in one last story?" Bolan asked.

"Very well," Indio said loosening his grip as he stood up, making sure to keep his position over Bolan. "You amuse me, government man. I grant you life long enough to continue doing so. For a moment, at least."

"There are men all over the world," Bolan said, "who think fighting has rules. Who think there is a 'right way' and a 'wrong way' to engage in combat with another human being. Some of them are martial artists. Some of them are athletes. Some of them are idealists. What they all have in common is that they expect others to conform to their expectations. Do you follow me so far?"

"I think I do."

"What none of them understand," Bolan went on, slowly inching in a circle beneath Indio, who kept shifting to face him, "is that when I fight a man, I don't care what his goals are. When two athletes or martial artists fight, they have symmetrical goals. They both want to win. They want to win according to some contrived set of rules, which determine what they can and cannot do."

"Yes?" Indio said, growing impatient. "What is the point of this? Hurry and tell me, because I am going to kill you."

"When I fight a man," Bolan said, "I care only about his defeat. There are rules I follow, Indio, but when a man has earned deadly force from me, all other restrictions are null and void."

"Yes? So?" Indio demanded.

"A famous author named Samuel Clemens once said that if he were ever challenged to a duel, he would kindly and forgivingly lead his enemy by the hand to a quiet place and kill him."

"This is the point of your story?" Indio asked.

"Almost," Bolan said. He looked up at Indio, judged the angle and decided it was safe. He added one more word: "Reaper," he said.

Four thousand rounds per minute, fired from an electric minigun attached to a Cobra gunship, blew the top half of Indio into a thick, red fog.

Epilogue

Mack Bolan looked up at the Lincoln Memorial. He supposed a more cynical man might fail to be moved by such an edifice. He, on the other hand, was always impressed by it. Wonderland, as Hal Brognola called it, was truly awe-inspiring. Even knowing the graft and corruption that lurked beneath its surface, even understanding how flawed were the men and women who walked the halls of power, Bolan was impressed by what this place represented.

He checked his wristwatch. Time. Time passed for all of them. The years slid by, the battles passed. How much time would any one of them get? It was impossible to say.

It wasn't Hal Brognola who was late; Mack Bolan was early. The soldier was always early for their meetings. He showed up in order to reconnoiter the situation, make sure there were no hostiles lying in wait. Brognola was a known man in Washington, and while few were certain precisely what the big Fed did, the man was a tempting target to some nonetheless.

The recent attempt on Brognola's life amply illustrated that.

Price had told Bolan about it during his initial debrief by sat phone. The hit man had been traced back to Eli Berwald. The motive was clear enough, if one allowed for the possibility that Brognola was known to command men like Mack

Bolan. Berwald had obviously made the connection and decided that Brognola was ultimately responsible for Aaron's death. There were any number of ways Lantern could have learned about the presence of "Matthew Cooper" and his interaction with Aaron's team at Nitzche's bunker in Kansas. The most obvious of these was the leak from within Lantern itself.

The soldier's thoughts were dark. This mission had been characterized by so much death. Thoughts of mortality, of every man's ultimate end, weighed on him. Bolan had no doubts, no regrets, about how he had chosen to live his life or fight his war. He was, however, aware that he had only a finite time on this earth. He would fight on for as long as he was able, but there would come a time when even he would be dead.

Every man was mortal. Every man walked into battle knowing that he might not walk off again.

The Spartans were said to have had a fatalistic attitude toward death. Dying in battle they could abide. Dying without honor they could not. "Return with your shield or on it," went the saying. The idea was that, if a man's courage broke during battle, the first thing he would discard would be his heavy shield. If the man instead fought on and died in battle, his shield would be used to carry his body home.

Mack Bolan had no shield, but every day, he faced no less a prospect. Fight on and die with honor, or give in to the countless forces arrayed against him, against Stony Man, against Brognola.

In his satellite debriefing with Barbara Price, the full extent of Nitzche's atrocities had been discussed in florid detail. How any single human being, even a relic of the Nazi regime, could be so inhumanly evil defied imagination. Even for Bolan, it was hard to grasp, and he had seen every atrocity a man could visit on his fellow humans. He had seen wanton death. He had seen pointless destruction. He had seen cruelty and torture, had ended with mercy the lives of people so savaged by Mafia and terrorist interrogators that they could never live a life free of intolerable pain and isolation. The old Mafia torturers used to call the people whom they carved "turkeys." Bolan had always hated that term.

He wasn't normally so pensive. This mission, and encountering Klaus Nitzche, had made him thoughtful.

Bolan walked some distance to the hot dog stand that was Brognola's favorite. He was hungry and didn't suppose the big Fed would mind if he started without him. He was about to step up and place his order when he felt a pair of eyes on him. His sixth sense of combat alerted him to the danger.

The kid had his head shaved and wore a black bomber jacket, black BDU pants and steel-toed boots. The SS tattoo on his neck told Bolan at a glance everything he needed to know. The punk was a skinhead, a redheaded stepchild to neo-Nazis like Klaus Nitzche. He was glaring at Bolan as if he knew him.

"Yeah, that's right, I'm looking at you," the skinhead said with a sneer, when they made eye contact.

Bolan stepped away from the hot dog cart. "Walk away," he told the skinhead.

"You *are* him," the punk said, pointing a finger. "I saw you on the news. You're a cop of some kind."

"I'm not a cop," Bolan said.

"Then you're military," insisted the skinhead. "You were part of the raid that killed Klaus Nitzche, stopped him from rousting those Jew terrorists!"

"That's an interesting interpretation of reality," said Bolan. "And not at all accurate. Let it go, kid. I'm not in the mood."

"Listen to this guy," the skinhead said, laughing to his girl.

She was dressed more or less as he was, but had more tattoos, and a ring through her nose. "Man, they're all the same."

"Who's that, exactly?" Bolan asked.

"You know, people like you," said the youth with a smirk, poking his finger in Bolan's chest. "Jew-lovers—"

Bolan grabbed the finger and broke it.

The punk's girlfriend started to scream. Bolan let her. He drove the web of his hand into the reeling skinhead's throat, dropping him. Once he was on the ground, Bolan kicked him once, hard, in the ribs. The skinhead moaned in pain.

"I have a theory," Bolan said quietly, "and that is that if somebody took the time to beat the ever-loving hell out of scum like you every time you stepped out of line, you might not grow up to be the losers you become. Get lost, kid." He bent down and whispered into the skinhead's ear. "If I ever see you again, *I will kill you.*"

"Making friends, Striker?" Hal Brognola asked.

"Always," Bolan said.

"Funny how that sort of thing tends to follow you around. It's only going to get worse, at least for a little while. Your little foray into television news, even your profile," Brognola said, "is making my life more complicated. I've got the Farm on it, quietly deleting internet records. The news agencies in question have been persuaded to cooperate. We'll keep as much of a lid on things as we can. You might want to consider taking a vacation."

"Gladly," Bolan said. "Just as soon as the world refuses to shake itself apart for at least a long weekend."

"Point taken," Brognola said. "I hear Hawaii is nice this time of year."

"Barb said they caught the assassins Nitzche sent after that bounty hunter character?"

"Yes." Brognola nodded. "The guy even managed to work

the near-miss into a publicity coup. Landed himself a few more interviews to promote his business and his reality show."

"He's consistent. You'd have to give him that."

"I suppose," Brognola admitted.

"You holding up okay in the wake of your own brush with adventure and excitement?"

"I am," Hal replied. "But that's part of why I wanted to meet with you in person. It's good to catch up with you once in a while, old friend."

"I hear that. I have a favor I'd like to ask of you."

"Name it."

"Claire Berwald," Bolan said. "I know she's in trouble, legally. Weapons charges, reckless endangerment, and whatever else the prosecution might choose to throw at her."

"There's hell to pay for what she and Lantern were doing, and tried to do." Brognola nodded.

"I'd like it if the powers that be took it easy on her," Bolan told him. "I think she's suffered enough. I'd hate to see her punished for trying to do what she thought was right, trying to protect her family and her people, especially after losing both her brother and her father."

"I'll see what I can do," Brognola said. "I don't think it's an unreasonable request."

"Treat it as a cashed-in favor, if that will help."

"You're the national debt of accrued favors, Striker," Brognola said. "The U.S. government owes you a favor about a billion times over, by my conservative estimate."

"Fair enough." Bolan glanced back at the hot dog stand. "I don't know if I'm hungry, after all," he said, "but I could sure use a drink. Buy you one?"

"I'll take a rain check. I'm going to attend the wake for my friend Lars. You would have liked him, Striker. He was a stand-up guy."

"I know," Bolan said. "I'd be honored to accompany you."

"Great. My driver is waiting. It's a bit of a hike from here."

"Getting your exercise, Hal?"

"Something like that," Brognola said. "I've had an epiphany."

* * * * *

Don Pendleton's Mack Bolan

Oblivion Pact

White supremacists unleash an international terrorist campaign of mass murder.

When a firefight breaks out in Mexico, the blitz leaves countless dead and Apache gunships in the hands of an Australian self-made millionaire and the soldiers of his white supremacist group. This puts Mack Bolan in grim pursuit, as there is no doubt that World War III is the millionaire's ultimate goal. Bolan must use everything he's got to dispatch the enemy into eternal darkness.

Available September wherever books are sold.

TAKE 'EM FREE
2 action-packed novels
plus a mystery bonus

NO RISK
NO OBLIGATION TO BUY

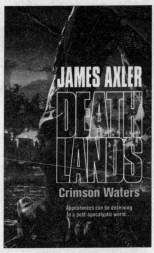

AleX Archer
THE MATADOR'S CROWN

Some men will do anything to win.

As somewhat of an expert on the medieval period, archaeologist Annja Creed jumps at the invitation from the Museum of Cadiz to assess its acquisition of Egyptian coins. She soon finds herself embroiled in a murder investigation that takes her through the colorful world of flamenco and bullfighting to a renowned matador and an illegal—and deadly—collection of Visigoth votive crowns.

Available September wherever books are sold.

www.readgoldeagle.blogspot.com

GRA38